Three hundred p[ ]
came hurtling a[ ]

...all of it aimed at Mack[ ]

The Executioner dived to one side. The brute went crashing into the wooden bedframe, smashing it to splinters.

Rising like a maddened bull, the terrorist lunged again at Bolan, grabbing a hunk of wood as he did so.

Bolan seized the man-mountain by the face, keeping the club away with all his strength.

Suddenly he rammed his forehead into the thick nose of the giant. Cartilage cracked noisily and a sticky spray shot out of the assailant's nostrils in a red flood.

Let his enemies beware: When The Executioner invades Germany, the hellrains turn to blood!

"America's most successful adventure series. The best in the business."

—*Navy News*

Other

MACK BOLAN

titles in the Gold Eagle
Executioner series

Mack Bolan's

ABLE TEAM

Mack Bolan's

PHOENIX FORCE

MACK

THE EXECUTIONER 46

BOLAN

Bloodsport

DON PENDLETON

A GOLD EAGLE BOOK FROM

WORLDWIDE

TORONTO · NEW YORK · LOS ANGELES · LONDON

First edition October 1982

ISBN 0-373-61046-7

Special thanks and acknowledgement from the author
to Ray Obstfeld for his contributions to this work.

Printed in Canada

Weep not that the world changes—did it
keep a stable, changeless state, it
were cause indeed to weep.
                    —*William Cullen Bryant*

Look abroad through Nature's range,
Nature's mighty law is change.
                    —*Robert Burns*

Take from me the hope that I can change
the future, and you will send me mad.
                    —*Israel Zangwill*

For sure, the world is changing.
Whether it's for good or for bad is
up to you and me. You and me, pal.
Let us try for good.
                    —*Mack Bolan, The Executioner*

This book is dedicated to the eleven Olympic athletes killed at Munich airport on September 5, 1972, by cowardly fanatics. We must not forget.

Joseph Romano	Weight lifter
David Berger	Weight lifter
Zeev Friedmann	Weight lifter
Yacov Springer	Weight lifting referee
Mark Slavin	Wrestler
Eliezer Halfin	Wrestler
Moshe Weinberg	Wrestling coach
Yosef Gutfreund	Wrestling referee
Andre Spitzer	Fencing coach
Amitzur Shapira	Track coach
Kehat Schorr	Marksman coach

PROLOGUE

For sure, the world had changed beneath Mack Bolan's feet. He had been born to a triumphal world, reared in a frightened one, matured in a confused one, plied his manhood in a threatened one. What was next? A dead world? An enslaved one? Or a world again triumphant and reaching once more for the stars?

Mack Bolan was no prophet, nor was he priest or politician. He could not preordain a world of justice, freedom and abundance for all—and he was not sure that he would if he could. Bolan was a soldier, with a soldier's understanding of moving forces. He knew that the planet earth had not been designed with Heaven in mind. It was a place for challenge and growth, a place where a force called Life raised awareness toward the stars and dreamed of rest—perhaps only because there is no ''rest'' in life, nor obviously had it ever been intended.

Things changed, sure. It had to be. Life was a

process, not a thing in and of itself, but a force moving inexorably along a pattern of continuous action. Process means change, yes, but change does not necessarily mean growth; it may also mean decay. . . or annihilation. This was Bolan's understanding and also a large part of his motivation. He lived now in a threatened world, a world almost literally torn apart by blind forces struggling violently toward a new order, a new stage for its actors, a new definition of "good."

There were currents and crosscurrents in that struggle, tidal pools and eddies—also "rock and shoals," as the navy called it—and Bolan knew the dangers were very real for this threatened world. He did not deal in personalities, in conventional moralities, in political nuances of right and wrong. This soldier dealt with a world in trouble, and it would not be a severe overstatement to say that he worked from a cosmic viewpoint. Some activities he perceived as beneficial, others as detrimental, to mankind as a whole. This remarkable warrior was not anti any person, group, cause or movement. He was pro world, and sought only to keep its changes forever positive and constructive, forever moving toward growth and away from decay and/or annihilation. It was, he knew, a struggle of cosmic dimensions.

One of the more troubling aspects for Bolan lay in the realization that some of those who would face him as antagonists would be as self-lessly motivated by the same concerns that moved him, but with different goals in mind. Bolan had always respected the true soldier who fights for his idea of right, "enemy" or not. He took no joy from the death of such men. But he also did not shrink from the call of his duty as he perceived it. He could respect and still kill the holy warrior of whatever persuasion who sought to dominate the world as a means of saving it. He did not and could not, however, find any respect in his warrior's heart for those who indiscriminately killed and maimed innocents and terrorized populations in the name of their "holy" cause.

The cause is defamed and the war debased when children are murdered as deliberate pawns for power, and Bolan has no stomach for those who proxied their battles onto safe streets against a defenseless "enemy," no matter what the cause or motivation. IRA, SLA, PLO or PDQ—whomever and whatever, these initial-ized would-be warriors who dealt only in terror and intimidation of civil populaces would find no stir of regret from the likes of a Mack Bolan should they ever rise into his gunsights; he would give them what they had bought by their own activities, and their blood would make no stains upon his soul.

The world had changed, yes, and so had Mack Bolan...but not that much. Not that much. The enemies of Man were still their own judges and their own juries...and Bolan was still their Executioner. Some things would never change.

1

Mack Bolan flattened himself against the dirty brick building and slid cautiously around the corner. The narrow garbage-strewn alley was oppressively dark. It smelled of urine and decay. Dank puddles from the morning's heavy rain still freckled the grimy cobblestones like pools of black ink.

The puddles nearest the main streets reflected shades of red neon. Each sign, in various stages of disrepair, was promising something just short of paradise.

Paradise, sure, Bolan frowned with disgust—that was the place where there was no morning after. But Bolan was not concerned with paradise right now. More like its opposite.

He held his breath a moment, listening for threatening sounds. There was nothing too unusual. Just the normal nightlife noises of too much drink and laughter that was too loud. Things that folks did to hide the too little happiness that goes with life in a dumpy hotel in a sleazy part of Frankfurt, Germany.

Bolan waited for a flurry of headlights to pass by before sticking his head back around the corner and waving briskly for the two MPs to follow. Seconds later he heard the clomp of heavy combat boots as the MPs jogged around the corner, splashing through the murky puddles, M16A1 rifles clutched in front of them.

They came expectantly to Bolan, young faces alive with determination to do a good job for the mysterious Colonel Phoenix to whom they had been assigned only a couple of hours before. Both had had less than two years' experience in the U.S. Army. But they knew enough to recognize a real soldier when they saw one. And they saw one in this Colonel Phoenix.

"Yes, sir!" Corporal Philo Tandy reported, snapping to attention. His trim blond hair peeked out from under his white MP helmet. He was very large and very young. "What next, sir?"

"Just as we planned it, Corporal," Bolan said, standing tall before them in his skintight black nightsuit. The .44 AutoMag was strapped to his hip. The 9mm Beretta Brigadier, with sound suppressor screwed tightly in place, rode snugly in the snap-draw holster under Bolan's left arm. Extra clips were tucked away within easy reach. Should he need them.

He hoped he wouldn't. Just a quick round-up operation. In and out with nobody hurt, that was the plan. Plans, of course, like people, have a way of unraveling on their own. . . .

It had been a tough probe right from the start, with no time for the usual precautions. Mack didn't like rushing in like some comic-book soldier, a grenade in each hand and a sub-machine gun clenched between his teeth.

Hell, he had hardly had time to change his fatigues from the Warco wipeout in the Ever-glades when Hal Brognola and April Rose cor-nered him during a quiet dinner at Stony Man Farm. Brognola had addressed him as Striker, and Bolan immediately knew something foul was in the wind. At the mention of his code name, his fresh four-inch wound earned in Algeria smarted as if in alert.

Information had come directly from the Defense Intelligence Agency, but not nearly as specific as Stony Man Farm would have liked—except for the timetable. Specifically, it was a now-or-never operation.

April and Hal had shown him photographs and filled him in on the few details they knew. Too damn few, and Bolan had complained about it at the time.

But in this business, damn few was sometimes all you got.

So it had to be enough. And this time it was. Certainly enough to send him packing, still chewing his porterhouse steak as Jack Grimaldi joined him to jet them both to Frankfurt. To stop a "business" meeting that must never take place.

Not if Mack Bolan could help it.

Bolan looked at the two anxious MPs assigned to him and grimaced. Corporal Philo Tandy was a baby-faced hulk from Tennessee who towered over Bolan like a cement wall. He had told Colonel Phoenix that he still dreamed of parlaying a Creek Bend High School MVP football trophy into an NFL halfback career, after he had paid his dues to Uncle Sam. Not dumb, Bolan knew, just a mite inexperienced in the ways of the world outside Creek Bend, Tennessee.

Not so his partner. Corporal Isaac Cleveland was a skinny, soft-spoken black man from Miami who had taken the trouble to learn German while stationed overseas and was now studying Russian. He was apparently not the kind of man to waste an opportunity: if he stayed in the army, Bolan realized, he would probably end up a general. And considering the mess that Bolan had been sent over to straighten out, the army could use a few more officers like Isaac Cleveland.

Okay, maybe they were not the toughest or most experienced MPs in the world, but they were the best General Wilson could come up with on such short notice. The general had huffed about security clearances for almost twenty minutes before Bolan had stopped him with a few choice words of his own.

It didn't matter to Bolan anyway. Tandy and Cleveland would do. They would have to.

"Listen close," Bolan snapped briskly, his voice all business. "This is a simple arrest. You've both done that before, right?"

"Yes, sir!" Corporal Tandy barked.

"I will go up the fire escape and block off the window. They cannot get out that way. Then you two go in the front door and arrest them. And keep your guns aimed and ready. These guys play for keeps." Bolan checked his watch. "I want you through the door at 0123. That's five minutes from now. Got it?"

Corporal Cleveland checked his watch. "Got it, sir."

"Okay, get moving. Remember, I want them alive. If possible."

"Yes, sir!" Corporal Tandy said.

Corporal Cleveland's eyes flickered with doubt. "Might be difficult, Colonel. What you told us about them..."

"If possible, Corporal," Bolan repeated. "If possible."

The two soldiers moved off into the darkness at a trot, dodging the puddles this time. They disappeared around the corner.

Bolan did not hesitate. He ascended the feeble old fire escape, its shaky vibrations rattling up his spine with each step. At the third-floor platform he squatted close to the wall. He pressed his face against the gritty brick. With fingertips spidering along the rough wall, the night warrior silently eased himself to the edge of the dirty hotel window, just far enough for him to see what was going on inside.

He did not like what he saw.

Three men in U.S. Army uniforms were sitting around a cheap folding card table. The one with the sergeant's chevrons was the high-ranker of the three; he was tipped back on his metal folding chair so that it balanced on its two wobbly back legs. The guy's big gut bubbled over his belt in a slab of lard, and a couple of bags of flab sagged down his cheeks into jowls. He was tossing playing cards one at a time across the room into his army cap. Bolan mentally searched the file of photographs stored in his mind since the mission briefing. He soon had the handle to match the face. *"Sergeant Edsel Grendal, pure one hundred percent USDA trash, weight exceeded only by greed,"* was Brognola's acrid assessment.

The other two "soldiers" were at least twenty years younger than Grendal's mid-forties. One was tall and gangly-looking, even sitting down. A PFC. He had straight red hair with a stubborn cowlick sticking straight up at the back of his head. Occasionally he gave it an absent pat, more out of habit than any real expectation it would lay down. He also had a nasty rash encircling his neck as if his skin were still too sensitive for shaving. He was shifting a good deal in his chair, blinking with nervousness.

The third man was a corporal, though he looked to be a year or so younger than the red-headed boy—unless you looked closely at the mouth: it was thin and bloodless, twisted into the kind of smug grin seen on a sadistic child setting fire to the neighbor's cat. The guy was slumped forward in his chair, staring at the paper napkin as he methodically shredded it into neat little piles on the table. The hard cruel mouth set in a weak, pasty face made the effect utterly demonic.

In the center of the table were seven or eight .45 M1911A1 handguns heaped together; also about two dozen clips of ammo. The young corporal dropped a few flakes of shredded napkin onto the pile of guns and snickered. "Look, Sarge, it's snowing in Germany."

Sergeant Grendal saw what the corporal was doing and sighed. Suddenly his meaty hand lashed out across the table and slapped the corporal's cheek in a hard-knuckled backhand.

"What the hell—!" the corporal cried, covering his cheek with both hands. "What'd you do that for, Sarge?" he whined.

Grendal leaned back into his chair again and tossed another card across the room. Ten of hearts. It dropped neatly into his cap. "You're fuckin' with the merchandise, boy. This ain't no *little* deal like you're used to makin' with your grunt buddies. This is big business with big bucks, and I don't want no shit-kicking punk like you treating it lightly. Get my meaning, boy?"

The corporal stayed sullen, still pressing his hands against a swollen cheek. Two small drops of blood trickled out of a nostril. He smeared them away with the back of his hand. "I didn't mean nothing."

The sergeant's voice was taunting. "You never do, Billy boy. So just try to sit still and be good like Gary here. Right, Gary?"

The redheaded PFC smiled weakly. "R-right, Sarge," he stammered.

Bolan felt rage throb thickly into his brain.

These "soldiers," especially the bloated Sergeant Grendal—they were prepared to deal in the death and terror of innocent victims for nothing more than a handful of paper dollars. Bolan cursed such people even more than the actual terrorists themselves, because cynical bastards of this ilk did not even have a phony political slogan to hide behind. Except "me first."

And before his eyes here, they were wearing the uniform of the United States Army. Mack Bolan was aware that to some soldiers the uniform was just an outfit you had to wear, nothing more. But to the Executioner and a few damn good men he knew, the uniform meant a million things more. Symbolic, in a word. It meant you stood for something good and right and you were ready to show the world you'd do anything to protect certain important and self-evident values. To Bolan it should always be that you could take one look at such a uniform and know that the man or woman in it had a code of honor and justice that would not ever be compromised.

And the big guy had seen too many of his buddies spill their guts into the stinking swamps of Indo-China in defense of their uniform and what it stood for to let scum like this dishonor it. That was going to cost them.

Yeah. They were gonna pay that price in full.

Bolan checked his watch again. Fifteen seconds left. He unsnapped the Beretta and slipped it out of its holster. The solid weight felt, as usual, appropriate in his hand. Good and right.

The muscles in his legs tensed like coiled snakes as he rocked onto his toes, waiting.

The loudest sound to him now was the thumping of his own heart, so anxious to act.

As he counted off the final three seconds, he felt the predictable cold spurt of adrenaline spearing through his stomach.

2

Three.

Two.

One.

Go! Go! Go!

Bolan sprang through the closed window, an unleashed, lashing-out body of muscle. His head was tucked down. His Beretta was tight in his right hand.

Glass exploded everywhere. Bolan had burst into the room like some avenging angel, or devil. The startled men at the table gasped in shock and horror. The violent appearance of the warrior with the black grease smeared over his face, his shape all clad in black, was the coming of their fate.

As planned, Bolan's action had distracted them long enough to allow Cleveland and Tandy to bust open the hotel door and cover the three prisoners with their rifles.

"Don't move!" he heard Corporal Cleveland command.

Sergeant Grendal was first to recover. Aware of what grim punishment the army would have in store for him now, he obviously decided to take a chance. A desperate chance.

He slammed his chair forward to the floor and grabbed at one of the guns on the table, snapping in a magazine with his palm. It took only a couple of seconds for the two MPs to pivot their rifles directly in the fat sergeant's direction, but by then too much else was already in motion.

Taking his cue from Grendal, the pasty-faced corporal vaulted out of his chair like a damn fool and lunged at the throat of Corporal Cleveland. "Black sonuvabitch—" he shrieked.

Corporal Cleveland swung his rifle butt up and into the smooth face of the flying corporal. It caught the soldier squarely in the open mouth and jaw. The jaw broke with a crack like it was some cheap plastic toy. The whole anatomical mechanism twisted too far to the left and white splinters of bare bone poked through the cheek's skin. Several blood-drenched teeth had exploded from his mouth and the dumb corporal tumbled into a heap of convulsions against the folding metal chair. His coughing sprayed a pink mist of bloodied phlegm out from his face and onto his shirt.

Corporal Tandy, diligent of Bolan's command to take these creeps alive, was meanwhile attempting the same rifle butt technique on Sergeant Grendal. But Grendal was combat trained, and despite his bulk he easily side-stepped the inexperienced MP, deftly clubbing the younger man on the back of the head with the butt of his just-grabbed pistol. Then with brazen expertise, he swung around to face Bolan, and squeezed off several rounds from a two-fisted crouch position.

But Bolan was not a sitting target.

From the moment he had plunged through the window he had kept moving, rolling across the wooden floor and its new carpet of glass shards to a better vantage for return fire. He heard the loud report of the .45 as he came out of his roll, saw dust and splinters kicked up from the floor before him as the sergeant's bullets dug in.

Bolan heard the third shot and felt a tug at his pant leg, enough to know it had been too damn close.

He twisted around, gaining enough leverage to dive behind the hotel's torn overstuffed chair near the corner. Halfway through the dive, he squeezed off two rounds of his own. The Beretta spat its smoldering chunks of brimstone into the fleshy neck of Sgt. Edsel Grendal. The hard-guy's throat burst open like a water balloon, pouring forth crimson blood over his chest and fat stomach.

Grendal reeled for a moment, desperately wrapping his hands around his throat like a tourniquet and choking out some rasping words of protest. But the blood merely pumped out between his sticky fingers as he collapsed face-forward into the card table, knocking it over. The guns and ammo clips rattled across the floor.

It was not over yet. Bolan continued his roll out from the other side of the chair, beading the Beretta toward the last soldier. The wretched redhead stood in the far corner, his hands already raised high over his head. "Jesus," he was saying. "J-Jesus goddamn. . . ."

Bolan rose slowly to his feet. There was no way anyone could mistake the shots from those M1911A1s as anything else but gunfire. However, it was doubtful that anyone would come snooping around. Especially the law. It was that kind of hotel, in that kind of neighborhood—it had been built in the 1600s to house the finest Dutch banking firm in the land, but times had changed and now all of this section of Frankfurt was frequented by anyone with a few bucks to spend on the dirtier pleasures. Especially bored young American soldiers killing time. The police avoided the area. There was no need to worry about the noise.

The Executioner had other things to worry about.

He approached the redheaded kid. "You PFC Gary Cottonwood?"

"Yes, sir. Cottonwood. T-t-that's me."

Bolan poked the corporal aside with the barrel of the Beretta as he stepped toward the slumped Corporal Tandy, just now coming back to consciousness.

"How's the head, son?" Bolan asked.

Tandy rubbed the back of his neck, rolling his head slightly to bring himself to alertness. "Fine, Colonel. I'm fine."

"I want you to take your prisoner—" Bolan pointed Belle at the face-wrecked corporal on the floor "—back to the base and lock him up, and tell General Wilson what happened. He'll know what the hell I need."

"Yes, sir. What about him, sir?" Corporal Tandy asked Bolan, glancing over the body of Grendal toward PFC Gary Cottonwood.

"I'll be bringing him along myself. After I ask a few questions."

At that, the doughy-faced victim on the floor tried to shout a threatening warning at the redheaded Cottonwood, but anything that came out through the mashed and mangled jaw was badly garbled. Two more teeth fell from his mouth and bounced across the floor.

"I hope you like oatmeal, Corporal," Bolan said. "Because you're gonna be eating it for a whole lot of months to come. Now get him out of here."

Corporal Tandy hesitated. "Sir?" he asked in a quiet voice.

"Yeah?"

"I'm sorry, sir. I mean about not taking them all alive and everything. It was my fault, I know."

"Like hell it was," Bolan grunted. "Grendal knew he was facing a firing squad or worse. He was bound to take his shot, no matter how bad the odds. Had nothing to do with you. You understand?"

"Yes, sir. Thank you, sir."

"Now move out."

"Right, sir!"

Then they were gone, and Bolan turned a hard eye on the frightened private. Nudging aside Sergeant Grendal's corpse with his foot, he freed one of the overturned chairs. He set it in the middle of the room and sat down, his Beretta still aimed at PFC Cottonwood's chest.

Cottonwood swallowed, his Adam's apple bobbing tightly in his throat. "S-sir?"

"Yeah?"

"May I sit down please? Otherwise...."

Bolan pointed his gun at the floor. "Sit."

Cottonwood sat and waited silently.

"Are you glad to be alive, Cottonwood?"

"Y-yes, sir."

"Well, don't be too glad, because it may be a very temporary situation."

"I see, sir."

"I'm going to give it to you straight, and then you're going to give it to *me* straight."

"Yessir."

Bolan stared icily into the boy's eyes. "You're the one who passed on the report about this location and the meeting to the authorities. Right?"

"Yessir."

"Why? And don't waste my time with rationalizations or excuses."

"No, sir, I won't." Cottonwood swallowed something thick in his throat. "I work the VT-100 computer terminal for incoming shipments of everything from toilet paper to tanks. Sergeant Grendal approached me a couple months ago with his idea of how to program the computer so that it kicked out certain supply orders as duplicate shipments. Hell, CFU is the most common explanation for anything that goes wrong over here."

"CFU?"

"Computer foul up."

Bolan nodded.

"Whenever we showed a duplicate supply of something, we had orders to crate and store the supplies in the warehouse, because you never knew when the CFU would go the other way and short us. That was General Wilson's idea. Once you got something, never return it. He'd always say that. It was Billy Tomlin's and Sergeant Grendal's job to crate the stuff and store it. Except that they started to sell the stuff on the black market."

Bolan leaned forward, his eyes boring into the nervous private like a laser beam through the neocortex.

"It was just small stuff at first...food mostly...then auto parts...then..."

"Weapons." Bolan finished the halting sentence for him.

"Yeah," the private said, uselessly.

Bolan stood up, his gun still aimed at the kid's chest. "So what happened to you? Lose your guts and decided to fink out on your buddies? They weren't cutting you in for enough of the take? What's your story, kid?"

PFC Cottonwood looked up. His voice was clear for the first time, his eyes even. "I know this might be hard for you to believe, sir.

Especially now. At first I *was* in it for the
money.... You know the horror stories about
how hard it is to live over here on what we're
paid. Especially if you're married, like I was
planning on doing this summer. So the money
looked good in the beginning. But then I didn't
like it anymore. I didn't. Like I said, you probably won't believe me, but so what."

Bolan glared at the soldier who was fast
becoming defiant as he unburdened himself of
his confession. He might make a good soldier
yet.

"Your report said the meeting with the Zwilling Horde was set for tonight."

"Yes, sir." PFC Cottonwood looked at his
watch. "They're supposed to show up here in
another three hours, at 0430."

"Aren't you guys a little early for the meet?"

Cottonwood nodded. "The sarge had never
met these people face-up before, so he was a
little anxious." The young soldier shivered in-
voluntarily amid the unscheduled wreckage that
surrounded him.

"Besides, the sarge didn't trust us out of his
sight. He was afraid Billy would go off and get
drunk or laid and not show up."

"Come on, guy," Bolan said, waving him to
his feet.

"Where to, sir?"

"In less than three hours, killers in the butcher class, some of the most bestial in modern history, true man-eaters are going to be coming through that door. And I am going to be ready for them."

Bolan's lips twisted into something less than a smile.

PFC Cottonwood was simply very glad that he would no longer be numbered among those about to be on the wrong side of this man.

No way could he stand it. The sprung tension that emanated from the blacksuit was like all of America's destiny coiled within one single individual.

The misguided but well-meaning private was enacting a surrender he had had in his mind as soon as the night-garbed apparition had come hurtling through the window. He knew instantly he was in the wrong league. The explosion of the window still sounded in his mind behind the sharper reports of the killing that followed it.

This big stranger clearly embodied more than the vast majority of men could hope to enact in a lifetime. He seemed to represent—in his presence, his manners, his dark and profound look—the manifest destiny that no longer could be spared on the frontiers of the American West but which was a gift to the Old World now, to tame and to teach the primitives of a new generation who should know already that the lessons of American history are written in blood.

PFC Cottonwood was only too happy to give in to that history and be accountable, at least, for his own blood. He would watch this stranger with manifest *awe*.

And he would serve him if he could.

3

April Rose hovered over the Diablo 1650 printer as it spat out information, printwheel clattering across the paper like a machine gun. She read each line twice, then shook her head grimly.

She reached over and picked up a stack of the accordion paper and let it unfold to her feet as she scanned quickly for something encouraging. But all she could do was shake her head again. It was getting worse and worse.

Someone unfamiliar with operations at Stony Man Farm might take one look at her and wonder if some fancy glamour magazine was shooting a special fashion layout. Maybe a Hollywood film crew was shooting a scene for a high-class thriller? Why else would such a beautiful young woman be isolated out here in Shenandoah Country with her finger on the pulse of international terrorism. . . .

But April Rose had her finger on a pulse much more important to her personally. The pulse of Mack Bolan.

At the other end of the communications room a door was flung open and Hal Brognola marched in. "Any word yet from Striker?"

April shook her head, continued reading.

"Damn," Brognola muttered. He patted his jacket for a cigar and finding none, looked over April's shoulder at the TeleCom data.

The big fed laid a gentle hand on April's shoulder. "Don't worry, he'll call in."

She forced a smile. "He'd better. He absolutely needs this new information before he proceeds. The whole plan will have to be changed."

"The whole thing stinks," Brognola decided gruffly.

He looked at his watch and felt a thin layer of sweat spreading across his forehead.

It was already ten minutes past Striker's contact time. There were a lot of reasons for Colonel John Phoenix to be late, including the one that neither of them would mention but both of them feared. Brognola took a deep breath and patted his pockets again for a cigar, still coming up empty.

No, nothing could have happened to the big guy. Not now. Especially not now, after what they had just discovered about the Zwilling Horde. As the White House liaison on this project, Brognola had already been in touch with the president. Even the Man was worried, insisting that the ex-fed handle the situation as promptly as possible and as quietly as possible.

So Mack Bolan had better damn well be all right. Most of all because Brognola and Bolan were friends. One ex-FBI agent in a three-piece suit who looked like the vice-president of IBM, and one black-clad warrior reeking of sweat, cordite, combat. An uneasy friendship, sure, but powerful and deeply committed.

An electronic buzz sounded. Half a dozen bright colored lights flashed across the telephone console. April ran over, clamped the headset over her ears, began flipping switches. These feed lines were the same as used in the White House; once the caller connected with the console, the conversation could not be tapped through the lines. She gestured at the spare headset which Brognola donned immediately.

"Striker?" Brognola growled. "You copy?"

Bolan's voice was clear. "You know, that's just what my high school teacher asked me when I got an A on my history exam. . . ."

April Rose sighed with relief. "Where are you calling from, Mack?"

"General Wilson's office. This place has been swept for bugs every day for the past five years, so the line should be secure."

Brognola forced the issue. "What happened with Sergeant Grendal, Stony Man?"

"Out of business. Permanently. So too his partner, Corporal William Tomlin. Our informant is on ice."

"You...okay?" April asked quietly.

"Fine. Snagged my pants on a sharp bullet, that's all."

"I'll mend it for you," she offered.

"I didn't know you gals did that kind of work anymore," Bolan responded warmly.

"On special occasions. For special people."

"Knock it off, you two," Brognola growled. "I have to advise you, Striker, that the situation is a lot different than we first envisioned."

"Different how?"

"Bigger."

"I'm listening."

"Much bigger. All of this has all been hush-hush for the past two weeks, even from me, till the intelligence boys got the clue as to what was going on."

"What the hell's up, Hal? Spit it out."

"Kidnappings. All over Europe."

"Who's been snatched?"

"Well, that's the kooky part."

"Athletes," April said. "Professionals from all different countries. Babette Pavlovski..."

"The gymnast who defected from Czechoslovakia two years ago?" asked Bolan, his voice strong, direct.

"That's the one. She's been touring Europe as a coach with the American gymnastics team. It's not yet known by the press, but she disappeared one night two weeks ago."

"Retaliation maybe. Those guys don't much care for defectors. Bad public relations. . . ."

Brognola negated that. "She's not an isolated case, Stony Man. The Olympic skier Udo Ganz didn't show up last Tuesday at his job with a Munich insurance office. Hasn't been seen since. Mako Samata, a martial arts champion with a chain of studios across France, taught an akido class at his Paris studio two weeks ago, then disappeared without locking up. Clifford Barnes-Fenwick, a top archer from Wales, was supposed to meet last week with his estranged wife to discuss their impending divorce. He never showed up. When she went to his apartment, she found it torn apart."

"Keep spilling," Bolan's voice commanded.

"You're not going to like it," Brognola said. "We've had two identifications. Witnesses positively identified from photographs a man seen at two of the kidnapping sites. Thomas Morganslicht."

There was three thousand miles of long-distance silence.

Then Bolan spoke. Quietly. His mind was already locked onto the problem. "Thomas

Morganslicht, number one creep of the Zwilling
Horde. The same group coming tonight to buy
our army's stolen weapons.''

"The same.''

"Don't forget his twin sister, Tanya,'' April
cut in. "*Zwilling* is German for gemini, twins,
right? She's as much the leader as he is. And
just as deadly. Some say deadlier.''

"The assignment has changed,'' Bolan said
simply.

"I guess,'' confirmed Hal Brognola. "Originally we expected you only to stop the arms sale,
thus crippling the Zwilling Horde as much as we
were able to at the time. But now the ante has
gone up. We have to find out *why* they kidnapped those sports people so many days ago,
and we must free them if at all possible. But
whether that is possible or not, you have to stop
whatever the Zwilling Horde is planning. Stop
them for good, Striker.''

"There's only one way to get that far,'' he
said casually.

"I know.''

"Means I'll be out of contact for a while.
Don't know how long.''

"Am aware,'' muttered Brognola.

"I'll have to get going,'' Bolan concluded in a
low voice. "Company's coming in a couple
hours.''

"Anything you need, guy?"

"Just your good wishes, Hal."

"All the way to hell," Brognola growled.

Bolan laughed softly, then broke the connection.

"Good wishes," April Rose whispered into the empty line.

Brognola nodded silently. The hellrains were due to fall once more, in Europe, tortured continent of oppression and endless centuries of war. Mack was in the pits of the earth again, back where hell reigned triumphant over failed politics and broken economies and badly divided societies.

Back to where hell was real—daily, and endlessly. Back to where he *had* to be, if the torrential terrors of our modern times were to be stemmed before the murky tide drowned reason again, as it had over there in the two big ones this century already.

Back to where things were supposedly so civilized.

Like hell.

Sophisticated weapons were being stolen from the U.S. Army in Germany. Some of these weapons were in the hands of terrorists. And now kidnappers. Evil creatures out to make an international reputation for themselves—at the expense of thousands of lives, and at the expense of the reputation of the United States Army stationed overseas.

Bolan would trace this rampaging wrong to its wretched source. And then there would truly be hell to pay.

In the shape of the Executioner.

4

Mack Bolan sat hunched over the scarred folding table, his eyes closed, his lips puffing loosely in a half-snore. The .44 AutoMag lay flung on the table with its clip empty and removed, the 240-gram bullets scattered across the tabletop like toppled toy soldiers. Next to his resting forehead was a cluster of empty brown bottles of Grolsch Dunkel Bier.

A floorboard creaked outside his hotel door.

Bolan's hands, hidden beneath the table, tightened in anticipation. He snored a little louder.

A faint scratching noise at his door.

Come right in, yeah. The water's fine.

In a building this old, it was hard to move silently. The floorboards groaned in protest at every movement. They sagged from the slightest weight.

The thick oak door was probably more than a hundred years old. It would not take long for whoever was outside to pick its single-tumbler lock. Any second now.

Bolan's cold eyes made one final sweep around the room to make sure everything was in order. The table and chairs had been picked up, the window reglazed, the blood scrubbed from the walls and floor, the body hauled away. All done secretly, efficiently, by a special squad of General Wilson's men. The General had thought it was the least he could do. Bolan had agreed with him. The U.S. Army was faced with potentially one of its most embarrassing moments. Bolan felt the hot stale air from the hallway as it rushed in. The air from the hallway smelled like fried haddock, while the air inside the room stank of cheap booze. He'd made sure of that.

As the footsteps approached him, Mack Bolan decided he was ready.

There were two of them. One set of footsteps belonged to someone who could afford to lose some weight, maybe twenty or thirty pounds. No matter how quiet he tried to be, Bolan could hear him like he was a charging tank.

The other set of footsteps belonged to a woman. Of that he was certain. There was a lightness in the sound.

Then a shadow washed across his face and Bolan knew she was circling to face him. He had arranged the old goosenecked lamp in the corner to shine on his face for effect. He continued to snore like a passed-out drunk, waiting for them to make their move.

A large hand with huge stubby fingers grabbed his hair, jerked his head sharply back, and a small knife blade was pressed against his throat. Bolan felt the cool steel's pressure against his windpipe, but still he kept his hands hidden under the table.

"What the goddamn—" Bolan spluttered, his eyes blinking open and shut.

His head bent back, he could see the woman standing in front of him, and the 9mm Firebird automatic in her hand. It was pointing directly at his forehead.

She was what the fashion houses called "classically" beautiful, except that she had an unusually deep cleft in her chin. She looked to be barely twenty-five, but stood calmly erect with the confidence of a much older person: someone who was used to controlling any situation and getting her own way. A tough lady. Her hair was long and black, with a sharp widow's peak that dipped low over her forehead. Bolan recognized her immediately from the photographs he had seen at Stony Man Farm.

Tanya Morganslicht.

She was beautiful, yeah, but she was also one of the two leaders of West Germany's most notoriously brutal gang of terrorists, the Zwilling Horde. They were responsible for kneecap shootings, bank robberies, and the torture and mutilation of the daughter of a wealthy American film star.

Beautiful, sure. Like a coiled cobra.

Bolan's hands twitched anxiously under the table. Now was his chance to rid the world of one of its worst leeches.

A few silent, controlled breaths brought him under control. Timing was everything right now, and this was not the time. Not quite yet.

"Sergeant Grendal?" she said in a polite and educated English.

"Yeah? So?" Bolan mumbled.

She waved the gun scornfully at the empty bottles of German beer. "Is this how you conduct business of such importance?"

"You're half an hour early, doll," Bolan leered. "If you'd knocked, I could have splashed some water on my face. Climbed into my tux. Baked a cake."

She smiled through thin lips.

The beefy hardman behind Bolan laughed, his whole belly shaking against Bolan's back. But the knife remained firmly pressed against his throat.

"Say, honey," Bolan said, "can you tell Fatty here to take away the butter knife. I thought we were here to do business...."

She arched a long curving eyebrow in amusement. "This is the way Klaus and I *do* business, Sergeant. It ensures that we have your undivided attention. And cooperation."

Klaus's belly jiggled against Bolan again.

Bolan snapped his hands up from under the table. One swift move. His right hand was wrapped around an apple-green RGD-5 anti-personnel grenade.

His left hand instantly plucked out the detonating pin. The knife at his throat pressed slightly harder.

"Now," Bolan said with cold menace, "this little baby holds a mere 110 grams of TNT. More than enough to shred all three of us into very lumpy dog food. If I so much as belch, my hand will slip off the safety lever and that would end the beautiful relationship we're building here. Your move, lady."

He could see she did not care one way or the other, that she thought the whole scene was ridiculous, but the knife at his throat twitched closer to puncturing the skin. Bolan knew what fat Klaus was thinking: Could he make it to the door between the time he slit Bolan's throat, the subsequent and immediate release of the safety lever—and the explosion.

"Forget it, Klaus," Bolan snarled. "This pineapple has a three-point-two second delay. Your hand won't even reach the door. Not attached to the rest of you it won't."

Bolan lifted the grenade higher. "Now back off, both of you."

The Executioner stared icily into Tanya Morganslicht's smooth and untroubled face. Her expression was still calm, with perhaps a little curiosity in it now. But she showed no fear whatsoever.

"Klaus," she nodded slightly.

Klaus hesitated. He didn't like this at all. They were supposed to be here to intimidate the big American, all the better to negotiate business terms. But the Ami had tried a trick out of their own arsenal. It was an insult—not to the cause, which Klaus cared nothing about, but to himself.

And for that the American would pay. Perhaps not at this moment, as Klaus had no desire to die. And of course they had come here to buy weapons, therefore they needed the soldier. But later he would get even. Permanently.

"Klaus," Tanya repeated. The knife was reluctantly withdrawn from Bolan's neck.

"Naechstes mal," Klaus mumbled.

"There won't *be* a next time, pal," Bolan said, standing up. "Not if you want to live to stuff your fat face with more bratwurst. Drop your weapons on the table in front of you, please. Do it now."

Tanya placed her pistol on the table. Klaus glared at Bolan as he surrendered his Swiss Army knife and a matching 9mm Firebird.

Tanya laughed as elegantly as if they'd been at a cocktail party at some embassy and Bolan had just propositioned her.

Bolan shrugged. He replaced the pin in the grenade and quickly snatched up Klaus's Firebird. "Now that we've got that out of the way, let's talk business. Money."

Tanya gestured at the metal chairs. "May we sit down?"

Bolan lowered himself into his chair. "No."

"Very well then. Let us talk business. You seem to have—how do you say it?—set us up quite efficiently this time?"

"Efficiency," Bolan said, maintaining in his attitude the role of Sergeant Grendal. "That's something we learned from you people. So is the old live-grenade trick that you popularized when hijacking planes. Like you, I'm a cautious person. I like to know the people I do business with. It saves me from a knife in the back or maybe a bullet from a military firing squad. This little scene has given me the chance to get to know you both better. And so far I'm not impressed."

Klaus took a step forward and Bolan tilted the automatic toward him. "See what I mean. Tubby here is a hothead. This is business, and I don't like doing business with hotheads. *Verstehe*?"

"Yes, Sergeant," she smiled, placing a restraining hand on Klaus's arm. "Please not to worry, we are as anxious as you are to do business. May we proceed?"

Bolan looked at Klaus, saw a face contorted with hate. Lips were drawn tightly over teeth in a vicious sneer. Klaus had been humiliated and he would get even, that much Bolan knew. In fact, he was counting on it.

"What have you got?" Tanya asked.

"A bunch of stuff," Bolan said nonchalantly. "A few 7.62mm M219 machine guns with matching XM132 tripods. Three 40mm M203 grenade launchers."

"Colts?"

"They're the only ones who make those babies. I've also got a couple cases of these RGD-5 grenades and some .45 caliber M3A1 submachine guns. And much more. Still interested?"

"Yes," Tanya said simply.

"I can get a variety of specialty items, too. Gas masks, flame throwers, a couple of RPG-7 portable rocket-launchers—that's with a 3.3 caliber."

"We might have a use for them."

"Well, like I said, I can get almost everything. You tell me what kind of operation you've got in mind and I'll see what I can come up with."

Tanya's eyes darkened from blue to black. Her lips curled into a sneer as she snarled at Bolan, "My operation is of no concern to you. You have no business asking."

Bolan lifted his hands in appeasement. The role of Grendal was beginning to sear his spirit. "Cool it, lady. Ever heard of a sales pitch before? I don't care what your operation is, I'm just trying to make a dishonest buck, okay?"

Tanya's cheeks remained flushed with blood. "Continue, then."

Klaus listened to the conversation without hearing a single word. Instead he had spent the time concentrating on easing the flat throwing knife out of his forearm sheath. By barely rubbing it against his leg, he had pried it loose and could feel the cold Swedish 6C27 stainless steel against his fingers. As a child he had won a 20 DM bet by hitting a mouse with a knife at ten meters. This was even less. And he was no longer a child.

"Instead of jitterbugging around for a few hours," "Grendal" was saying to Tanya, "why don't you just tell me how much you can offer? That way we'll know if you're wasting my time. See, the army is going to be missing this stuff eventually, as I'm sure you can appreciate. And they tend to get really nasty about stolen armaments. Especially when it's their own soldiers doing the stealing. So I gotta watch my hide." The mimicry came naturally to Mack Bolan only from his years of observation of the world's true vermin.

Klaus eased the knife further into his palm. His wrist felt the black micarta handle as it slid into place. He casually shifted his hand behind his thigh to hide the blade's emergence. Soon, he thought, licking his lips. Very soon.

"I have a better idea, Sergeant Grendal," Tanya said. "Why don't you show us a few samples first as a display of what you call 'good faith.' Then we will talk money."

"And what kind of money are you talking about anyway?" continued Bolan. "Dollars, deutsche marks, Swiss francs?"

"Whatever you require."

She had taken the hook, and now he had to make her swallow it.

Bolan stood up and strolled casually to the window, his back to Tanya and Klaus. "That can be arranged," he nodded, rubbing his chin thoughtfully.

Now! Klaus screamed silently, swinging the knife over his head and throwing it with all his might at Mack Bolan's exposed back.

5

Hal Brognola arrived at the communications room in much the same manner he employed to bust down doors of Mafia kingpins. "I got your message," he barked at April. "What happened? What's so goddamn urgent?"

April's face was ghostly pale, whiter than he had ever seen it before.

"What is it, April?" Hal Brognola said, softly now.

April took a deep breath and straightened her shoulders, forcing her body to resume its professional stance. Her voice was crisp and steady. "Update reports on the preliminary investigation into the Zwilling Horde kidnappings. It seems NATO and the CIA teamed up on this one and sent a couple of agents undercover. A man-and-woman team."

"What did they find out?"

"No one knows."

"They haven't checked in yet?"

She shook her head slowly and handed him a page just torn from the printer.

As Brognola read, she could see his face change into an expression of disgust. When he was finished, he lifted his eyes to meet hers and shook his head resignedly.

"They discovered the bodies this afternoon, or at least what was left of them," April said. She was fighting against a quaver in her voice, determined to maintain her military demeanor. "As the report states, there is sufficient evidence to indicate severe torture, including castration of the man and rape of the woman. A sharp knife or razor was used on both, particularly around the face. Fortunately they were both dead before some of the other atrocities were committed, including the gouging of the eyes. Unfortunately, they were alive for the rest."

Brognola crumpled up the report in his hands and tossed it savagely into a corner of the operations room.

"Well, some men don't scare that easily," he said.

"You mean Mack doesn't," said April, the sadness in her voice an almost tangible thing. "You mean that Mack will ignore the demented actions of animals because the mission calls for nothing less. Hal, sometimes we ask Mack to go against every natural law there is."

"April, listen to me," said Brognola, attending to some of the paperwork that lay before him on top of the low computer cabinet, his head bent with a stubborn concentration on other matters. "Striker has had plenty of practice breaking the law these past ten years. Let's pray he can bend a few natural ones now that the circumstances require it. Enough said. Now back to our duties. I cannot bear to dwell on things that neither you nor I can bend at all."

April looked at her superior with impatient acceptance. Pray was right. Pray for a sane world and a job that did not lick at the salt of death. Such a world, such a job, could happen at any time.

Just as soon as hell froze.

Let us pray, she said in silence, for flames of ice and an end to war everlasting.

Could be that hell hath no fury like this woman's prayer. . . .

6

Klaus brought his arm down with the fluid motion he had perfected over countless similar moves. The knife left his hand, spinning toward Bolan's back like an airplane propeller that had broken free. To Klaus it was an ordinary mathematical equation: Knife leaving his hand equals dead man.

But Bolan was not an ordinary man. And this was far from the first time he had cheated fate.

Bolan exposed his back for only the fraction of a second he knew it would take Klaus to whip out and throw the knife. As the blade left Klaus's fingertips, Bolan dropped like lightning into a tuck, turn and roll. He heard the dull thud as the blade buried itself into the wall.

He came out of his roll with one knee to the ground and both hands gripped around the Firebird. Bolan squeezed the trigger twice and watched the front of Klaus's chest collapse. Klaus staggered forward, his upper body a growing jelly of blood. Bolan fired two more direct shots into the dying man's lung and kidney.

Then he swung the Firebird toward Tanya like a rigid finger of damnation. But she stood immobile, a bored expression on her face as Klaus crashed to the floor.

"Is this absolutely necessary, Grendal?" she asked petulantly.

"Hell, no," muttered Bolan, "not if I have no objection to a slice of steel sticking out of my back."

She stared at Bolan as the corpse at her feet bubbled blood in a pool between them. "Yes, well, I detest stupidity," she said with some difficulty. "And Klaus was stupid beyond my expectations."

"My view entirely," Bolan said with a bitter smile. He stood upright as his finger hovered teasingly over the trigger. He anticipated only a conciliatory move from her now, a furthering of their business deal. The killing here was done, most likely. Next was a play from her.

Tanya looked at her watch, then at Klaus's crumpled body. Dark shadows of anger washed over her face and Bolan thought she was about to spit on Klaus. But it passed quickly and she was all business once more. "All right, Sergeant. Let us go and inspect these arms you speak of. I must insist on that now." She walked over to the door and hesitated. "What about this fat pig?"

"I'll have one of my civilians come by with a body bag," said Bolan. "Money talks loud nowadays. Klaus will soon turn up in the Main River, the victim of a mugging."

She was already halfway down the hall when Bolan flicked the hotel room's light three times before closing the door.

Bolan had just created a hole in his enemy's organization. Now he had to make himself available to fill that hole.

A hellhole, that was for sure.

How cruelly she had helped him dig it.

7

"Hold it right there, sir," the man ordered, snapping his .45 automatic out of its side holster and aiming it at Mack Bolan.

"Easy, son," Bolan said from behind the wheel of the jeep. He kept his hands firmly planted on the steering wheel.

"May I see your identification, sir?"

"Sure thing, Corporal. Okay if I reach into my shirt?"

"Yes, sir," the young man said evenly. "But slowly, sir."

In the darkness, Bolan noted the other soldier standing inside the bulletproof checkpoint booth behind the corporal, grimly watching the action. The soldier's hands were below the booth's window. Without a doubt they were wrapped around an M3A1 submachine gun.

Bolan pulled a laminated slip of plastic from his pocket and handed it over. The corporal glanced back and forth between the photo on

the card and Bolan's face several times before
handing the card back.

"Sorry, Sergeant. Thank you for cooperating."

Bolan smiled. "What the hell's going on here
tonight? You fellas are edgier than a cat in a
room full of rocking chairs."

The corporal shrugged. He returned his .45 to
his holster, but left it unsnapped. "All I can tell
you, Sergeant, is what they told us. That all
guards are to be doubled until further notice.
No one goes in or out without a thorough check
of ID, no matter how well we know them. Even
General Wilson."

The corporal motioned to his partner in the
booth. The metal guardrail in front of the jeep
rose automatically and Bolan drove through
with a wave of thanks.

Immediately he pulled the jeep around the
corner of an old barracks building and parked
in the dark shadows. "It's all clear," he
whispered, quickly flipping back the rear seat.
Tanya Morganslicht took a deep breath, shook
her long black hair over her shoulders, climbed
out of the hidden compartment of Sergeant
Grendal's jeep.

"I heard what that soldier was saying to
you." Tanya climbed into the front seat, her
thigh brushing against Bolan's shoulder. Once

seated, she turned to face him with an intense expression of controlled anxiety. "It is never wise for me to come here, you understand that," she said.

Bolan shrugged. "Suit yourself, lady. I can take you out again right now, same way we came in. But this is where I keep my goodies stored and I ain't risking sneaking them all out of here on your maybe. If you want to buy them sight unseen, that's okay by me, too. But make up your mind."

Tanya's face twitched angrily. Bolan was out of the jeep before she could say anything. "This way," he whispered, motioning with his head.

She stayed close to him in commando formation, creeping forward or flattening herself against a wall at the instant that he did.

She was good, he realized, maybe too good to make this next part work.

He shook the thought from his mind and continued forward. It had to work. Everything depended on it.

"It's huge," she said at last, looking up at the massive metal building at the back of the army compound.

"It used to be an airplane hangar," Bolan told her, whispering in the darkness as she marvelled at the shadowy form that they approached. "But it was converted into a storage building about five years ago. I have my own private little corner in there that no one else even knows about. Come on.''

They jogged quickly across the paved street, Bolan in military uniform, Tanya in black jeans and sweater, then they crept toward the armed guard who stood semi-alert in front of the entrance. As the guard saw them he swung his rifle and took aim.

''Relax, Bendix, it's me.''

''Sarge?''

''Who else?'' Bolan looked around. ''I heard the guards had been doubled, where's your shadow?''

Bendix pointed with his rifle. ''Leadline's over there someplace taking a leak. Jeez, Sarge, I don't know—when Cottonwood offered a cut of this action, I had no idea what I was getting myself into.''

Bolan took a step toward him, his Beretta gripped firmly at his side. ''Now you know, wise guy. Any problems?''

Bendix swallowed hard and shook his head. ''No problems, Sarge. None at all.''

Bolan smiled menacingly at the stranger. ''I'm sure Cottonwood filled you in on the whole operation, right?''

''No, sir. He just told me I was to let you in.''

Bolan lifted the Beretta and tapped the soldier

on the chest. "Good. That was the right answer, son. You don't need to know anything more. Now let's get moving."

"Right, Sarge." PFC Bendix unlocked the small metal door inset into the main hangar doors and let Bolan and Tanya enter. He closed and locked the door behind them.

"Over here," Bolan said, aiming a small pocket flashlight, leading the way down huge aisles of stacked goods.

"My God," Tanya whispered, "this building must have everything. The things we could do with such equipment."

They came to a dark corner piled high with hundred-pound bags of what the powerful odor indicated to be fertilizer.

"Right here," said Mack Bolan.

"Here?" She surveyed the stacks of bags, piled to a height of fifteen feet on pallets. She guessed there were at least ten wooden pallets up to the back wall.

"Watch." Bolan grabbed a hand-operated dolly, slipped the metal prongs into the slots of one of the pallets, then dragged the wooden platform back. Behind it was pitch blackness.

"Generally the smell keeps most people away," Bolan told her as he started into the entrance.

Inside was wooden bracing separating and

supporting walls made up of hundreds of bags of fertilizer. The stench was staggering.

"It ain't much," Bolan said, "but I call it home."

She sighed wearily. "Can we get to business, Sergeant Grendal?"

Bolan handed the woman the flashlight, then hefted a crowbar and pried off the lid of a nearby crate. He reached in, pushed aside some packing material, pulled out a .45 M3A1 submachine gun. He held it at chest level for a second, smiled, then tossed it across the space at her. She caught it with one hand, nearly dropped it, regained her grip with both hands and examined it.

"This is different than the ones we have," she said, fumbling with the flashlight.

Bolan shrugged. "You might have some of the old M3s. The M3A1 is an upgraded version. It's a superior weapon."

She looked up from the gun and stared at Bolan in the fragmented gloom. "How so?"

He had a feeling she damn well knew the difference, was just testing him out. "First you'll notice the larger ejection port here. The old retracting handle's been eliminated. Also, this piece has got a finger hole for cocking and a larger oil can inside the grip. It's got a stronger cover spring, a guard added for the magazine catch, a stock plate and magazine filler added to the stock. She weighs eight pounds but can fire three-fifty to four-fifty rounds per minute at approximately nine hundred and twenty feet per second. Quite a handful. In the right hands.''

"It's nice,'' she said simply, laying the gun aside on top of a crate.

"Nice? You have a flair for understatement, lady.''

"What else do you have?''

"Pretty much what I told you before. Two crates of these M3A1s, a couple of the M1911A1 .45 pistols. I can get you grenade launchers within the week and probably some 7.62mm NATO machine guns by the end of the month.''

She shook her head impatiently. "Let's just talk about what you have right now, Sergeant. Here and now.''

"Well, I do have one particular item you might like.'' He disappeared behind two monolithic crates and came up with what looked like a laser gun out of some science fiction epic.

She gasped.

"Yeah, I knew you'd feel that way,'' he nodded, stroking the weapon. "It's a Heckler and Koch G-11 Caseless assault gun. This smooth exterior is a very tough plastic with the one-ex scope mount an integral part of the receiving molding. That makes the scope available as a carrying handle. And this little switch here allows you to go automatic to semiautomatic to single-shot.''

"It looks like something out of the future.''

"Yes, it does. But don't let its stream-lined looks fool you. This baby can deliver. Its magazine holds fifty in-line caseless cartridges, mounted right here in a horizontal bar along the barrel, extending all the way back to the receiver. There's no recoil and no bullet casings flying all over the place. Its caliber is four-point-seven times twenty-one millimeters and, in full automatic, it fires around one thousand rounds per minute.''

"Nice,'' commented Tanya distantly.

"The ammunition has a muzzle velocity approximately three thousand one hundred feet per second. And its ammunition uses a propellant whose cook-off point is one hundred degrees higher than the standard nitrocellulose powders which—''

She waved a dismissing hand. "Yes, yes, Sergeant. I am convinced of its usefulness. You may stop your sales pitch.''

"The base has a consignment of one dozen of these, but this is the only one that's gotten 'lost' so far. . . .''

Tanya Morganslicht glanced at Bolan with a special curiosity.

"You look and sound like a man who understands killing well," she said. Then her voice became hard again. "We'll take it, plus the rest. How much?"

All talk of prices was interrupted by the clatter of heavy combat boots, echoing under the metal roof. The shout of military commands fissured the still air.

"This is Major Thompson, Grendal," a deep voice hollered. "We know you're in here and we know what you've been up to. I have Cottonwood in my custody."

"Son of a bitch," Bolan muttered, extinguishing the small flashlight. Lights beyond their hiding place flashed all over the interior of the big building.

"What's happening?" Tanya whispered, her voice and features almost psychopathically calm.

"Oh, nothing—just that they know about us and what we're doing here and they're going to arrest us. You'll probably get thirty years in prison and I'll be shot sometime next week while trying to escape. That clarify the situation for you?"

"I must not be caught," she said urgently.

"Hey, I'm with you, lady. Now tell it to those

bozos. They get all mushy inside when they hear a sad story."

Bolan poked his head through the doorway, saw the men taking positions, ducked back in. "There's only one way out of this." He went back to the crates and picked up the Heckler and Koch G-11. He slapped in a magazine, then grabbed four square magazines and stuffed them into his pockets. "Here," he said, handing Tanya his Beretta pistol. "You use this."

"Why not give me one of the submachine guns? I can give better cover with one of them."

"Because I'm the one giving cover. You're the one running. The only chance we have is to blast a hole through them just big enough for us to make a break. Now let's go!"

The major's voice boomed again. "We know you're in that shithole. So come out here with your hands up. Now, soldier!"

Bolan stuck his head through the doorway again, the H & K clutched to his chest, the setting on full automatic.

A single shot echoed through the building and a bag of fertilizer two feet from Bolan tore open and spilled its contents onto the floor. Bolan ducked back in, took a deep breath, then ran through the doorway, his finger squeezing the trigger. The H & K sent forth a thunderous symphony of explosions as it chewed up wooden crates and popped fluorescent lights. Tanya Morganslicht did not have to be told what to do. She hunched low and dashed down the narrow alley of stacked crates. Bolan followed ten feet behind, spraying an arc of bullets to cut their way through.

A burst from a submachine gun kicked up wood and dust in their trail, but nothing came too close to them.

Until the exit door. Two guards stood side by side with .45s blasting at Tanya and Bolan. Tanya dropped to the ground, rolled once, and fired the Beretta twice. The soldier on the left threw up his rifle and sprawled forward onto his face. Tanya fired twice again from her prone position and the other soldier spun around and tumbled over a small hand truck.

Bolan dragged her to her feet as he ran by her. They came through the door, guns ready, but no one was waiting.

"This way." Bolan bolted across the street to the three parked jeeps that had brought the soldiers. Over his shoulder he heard men at the door of the building. Bolan swung around and blasted ten rounds at the doorway. There were cries of pain.

"Start it up," he commanded as the woman terrorist clambered into the lead jeep. Bolan fired more rounds at the door. He jumped into the jeep as it roared to life and lurched down the road toward the checkpoint booth.

He reached over and grabbed his Beretta from Tanya. "We'll need the silencer for this next part."

"Isn't it a bit late for stealth now, Sergeant?" she gasped in desperation.

It took the squealing jeep less than a minute to make it back to the checkpoint, the tires smoking the whole way.

The two men inside the booth jumped out at the sound of the tires, one with a .45 drawn and the other with his M3A1 at the ready position. They both took aim at the approaching jeep as it screamed to a halt twenty feet in front of them, the jeep's headlights shining in their eyes.

"Listen here, you men," Bolan shouted. "We're after two terrorists, two live ones. This is for real. One's a woman, the other's a man in a sergeant's uniform."

"Yes, sir!" one of them shouted back, his hand shielding his eyes from the lights. "We got the call."

"Okay, so watch it," Bolan said. The two guards lowered their weapons. Bolan's Beretta hissed. He squeezed the trigger four times. Both guards collapsed on the road. Bolan jumped from the jeep and ran into the booth, raised the metal gate, and leaped back into the jeep as it sped by. "Just keep following this road," he told Tanya. "We're about to steal home base."

General Wilson leaned across his desk and spoke into the intercom. "Buzz me as soon as you get through to that number. *Immediately!*" He clicked it off without waiting for a reply. He swiveled his massive leather chair around to face the two majors standing next to his desk.

"Is everyone accounted for?"

"Yes, sir," Major Thompson said.

"Injuries?"

Major Felder cleared his throat as if embarrassed. "Well, sir, two. Corporal Donner's trick knee went out when he was climbing the crates, and Private Simms skinned his elbow when he fell on the macadam."

"That's it?"

"Yes, sir."

General Wilson leaned back in his chair with a sigh. "Well, that's not too bad then. Not too bad at all."

The telephone buzzed and he snatched up the receiver. "General Wilson here. I'm calling in reference to Colonel Phoenix. That's quite all right...I understand the need for security. In fact, your Colonel Phoenix has taught me a

whole new lesson on that subject... Yes, we
followed his plan all the way.... Just a few
minor injuries.... No, I used my best marks-
men, or markspersons, I guess, since two of
them are women. They kicked up some
splinters, but never came close enough to harm
your man or his pigeon... Oh, he was a perfect
gentleman. We're going to have to replace some
lighting fixtures and doors, but otherwise he
kept the live bullets a comfortable distance
away. The woman's gun had the blanks, so he
let her do the actual killing.... Personally, I
thought my men overacted a bit, but I'm
assured they were quite convincing in fact....
Yes, I understand. No problem. Just one other
thing I'd like to say. That's a hell of a soldier
you've got there. A hell of a soldier... No, I
want to thank *you*. And him. If I hear any more
I'll be in touch. Goodbye.''

The general replaced the receiver and leaned
back into his chair. ''A hell of a soldier,'' he
repeated.

''Yes, sir,'' the majors chorused.

''Take that road,'' Bolan pointed.

''That's not a road,'' Tanya complained.
''It's matted grass.''

''Take it.''

She did. ''Where are we going?''

"It's your country," he grinned. "I thought you'd know."

"I'm not familiar with this area."

"Me neither, but I know this is the right way."

"How do you know?"

"Because it's taking us away from them." He hooked a thumb over his shoulder.

Tanya didn't smile. "That was a remarkable escape we made."

"Nothing that a dozen trained soldiers couldn't have done," he muttered. "You people still interested in this space gun here?"

She shrugged. "We might be for a few hundred deutsche marks. But what will you do now?"

Mack Bolan was of the opinion that the play-acting that she was an ignorant party to should be played for real, real soon, with her as target. But that would be too hasty. The charade must continue, at the risk of being discovered, or even, at any moment, of one of those soldier boys, civilians too, falling for it enough to shoot to kill. Until then, roles must be played out.

"Oh, hell, don't worry about ole Edsel Grendal. I've been taking care of myself for a long time," he said. "I'll be back in business within a couple of weeks."

"How? Now that you are out of the army, your supply line has disappeared."

"You think I'm the only one in this army who's been boosting goods? I know at least three others, including a colonel over in Wurtzberg. After the smoke clears, I'll be back again as a middle man between the sellers and the buyers. Taking my cut from both. Less work, less risk."

"What will you do in the meantime?"

"Well, first thing we do is ditch this jeep. If you have a couple of hundred marks cash, you can take this gun with you right now. Or we can meet sometime next week. Either way we have to split up now. They're looking for a couple, remember."

"True. But one phone call to my comrades and I will be underground within the hour."

"Congratulations."

"I can arrange transportation for you also, if you wish."

Bolan hesitated, as if thinking it over. "I don't know," he said. "I appreciate your offer, but there are more people looking for you guys than there are looking for me."

"You must make up your own mind. However, I should tell you that our people are in need of a weapons expert, and you have demonstrated your worthiness in that area. You are also available, I would guess, considering recent events.... You are an outlaw, like I am. And you are an extraordinary fighting man. I think we would be able to hide you out until—how did you put it? —the smoke blows up.''

"Smoke clears," he corrected her. "And what do you want in exchange? This H & K?''

She smiled thinly. "For now, Sergeant. For now."

"You've got yourself a deal, I guess. Nothing to lose."

The big man leaned back in the seat.

Nothing to lose.

Except life.

The kidnapped athletes awaited rescue. Life was more precious by the minute. He would surely not lose it to a hotheaded girl terrorist in the cobblestoned theater of Europe's current crisis. It was a crisis based on a very simple problem. If modern terrorism is not fought—and fought hard—people in the dwindling democratic and non-communist world will not have to wait for The Bomb. They will be blasted and ripped into submission on a daily, weekly, monthly, yearly basis. The problem being how to make the punishment fit that crime.

The premise is agreed—some murders are so horrendous that the most practical solution is to execute the perpetrators. Such murders are murders of perversion involving torture, sex slayings, contract killings, terrorist killings.

Why keep such people alive and in a cage for the rest of their lives or, worse, to be released when a mere two-thirds of their sentence is done?

But the difficulty arises when it is felt, especially in the older cultures, that the means of execution are barbaric. Hanging is horrible and unpleasant for those who have to do it, order it, witness it. The answer, for Europe, is The Executioner. The Executioner will not miss his shot to give a lady terrorist a better chance in the courts, to keep his hands clean of death. He could never fear death so much that he would sacrifice the possibiliy of a stronger, truer life.

No, he would value life, every minute of it, even as his Sergeant Grendal character tipped the play deeper toward death, finally to slip totally into hell and bring all the other evil parts sliding down with him to the darkest depth.

The role was his key to life. And death. The Morganslicht death.

8

A rifle butt thumped against the door.

"Ja?"

"They are almost here," the voice croaked. "Hermann saw the car. It is about a kilometer away."

"Danke," Thomas Morganslicht said, throwing off the blanket and staggering out of bed.

He pulled on a thick turtleneck sweater, jeans, hiking boots. The cabins were without any heat, except for the flickering fireplaces. He tugged the red knit cap over his shiny black hair, pulling it back on his head to allow the sharp point of his widow's peak to show. He liked the way its dagger appearance seemed to startle his men, almost intimidated them. As their leader, he desired every advantage over them he could get.

Morganslicht snatched up his gun and shoulder holster, shrugging into them as he walked out of the cabin. Several of his men stood around outside his door, their weapons in hand as they waited for the approaching Saab. The cool sun was peering over the tops of the snow-covered mountain peaks. The men kept moving, rocking back and forth, their breath steaming from mouths and nostrils.

"What time is it, Hermann?"

"Almost six-thirty."

"They must be very tired after their escape, and then driving all night." His voice was more amused than sympathetic. "And how are the prisoners doing?"

"Cold, but otherwise functioning normally," replied Hermann. "They no longer bother to complain."

Thomas grinned. "Good. I thought Rudi would convince them to accept their situation."

The giant called Rudi Blau turned his six-foot-six bulk toward them and chuckled damply through massive yellowing teeth. Bundled up in a long black coat and fur-lined hat, he looked like a mutant bear that had inadvertently stumbled into civilization. His eyes were small, too small even to determine their exact color, but his head was a huge round melon.

In his right hand he carried a hunk of firewood. He used it to persuade the prisoners to keep quiet. If need be he would persuade them into unconsciousness.

Thomas Morganslicht and his guards watched

the car puffing up the snow-covered road, its exhaust billowing around it like a pocket of fog. Hans Regens, who had driven all the way to Frankfurt to pick them up, was still driving. Tanya was next to him in the front seat. In the back seat, another figure—presumably the big American sergeant she had told him about in her communication. The unusual man who had helped her escape. A most independent being, by all accounts. Frightening.

Morganslicht frowned. He did not know this American, and he did not like him. It was perhaps necessary to have dealings with such people to get what the group needed, but they were dangerous and should eventually be eliminated. Especially men of such a scale and skills as this one. He had killed Klaus. . . .

Of course, Klaus had not been a very stable person. During the torturing of the two agents, he had not in fact been able to stop. Then it had been up to Thomas to show the proper way to mutilate the enemy, to extend the sport with skill, not lust.

But Klaus was dead and they were without enough weapons. So they would use this dumb American as much as possible, then kill him.

But slowly, maybe more slowly even than with those two damned agents. For demonstration purposes.

The car braked to a halt and the two front car doors opened at once. The driver, Hans, climbed out first, rubbing his neck to shake off the drowsiness of seven straight hours of driving. "The car needs a tune-up," he said, and walked off to get some hot coffee.

Tanya slid out next, offering a lingering look at her twin brother.

"Sergeant Grendal," Tanya called out, "we are here."

No response.

"Sergeant Grendal," the woman repeated loudly.

Still no response.

She pulled open the back door and ducked into the car, shaking Bolan by the shoulders. He appeared to open his eyes with a start, looking at her with a confused expression, then he yawned in her face. "Pardon me," he smiled brazenly.

"We are here, Sergeant," she said.

Thomas Morganslicht watched anxiously as the big man in army uniform leaned out of the car and unfolded to his full height.

It was a disturbing sight. The man seemed on the surface to be indolent, perhaps doltish, a typical problem for the army: he was a maverick, obviously, with some flaw within him, some indecisiveness of character no doubt. And yet. . . .

And yet behind that veneer of easy confidence and untroubled directness lurked another force altogether.

He could feel it on this chill mountain morning. It was a darkness. It was something disarmingly strong.

It was a visible danger emanating from this big man. Morganslicht did not like it at all.

9

Jack Grimaldi dipped the small helicopter down for a closer look at what the commotion was about.

He checked his map for bearings, decided he was about ten kilometers past Fussen, about ten from Garmisch-Partenkirchen. The Bavarian Alps stood like Prussian guards between the German and Austrian borders, looming impossibly high in the distance. He hoped he could locate Striker's signal soon. He had little desire to fight the treacherous, twisting air currents that swirled around those mountains. Except that Jack Grimaldi would do anything for Mack Bolan, and death be damned.

The Bell dropped five hundred feet in seconds, the better for him to get a closer look at the two men fighting in an open field.

One of the men stopped just as he was about to throw a punch into the face of the smaller man, and looked up at the helicopter. The smaller man did not bother to look up. He took advantage of the distraction to dig a sharp blow into his opponent's hefty stomach. The bigger man doubled over, clutching his middle, allowing the other to club him across the face with both hands clasped together.

Jack decided it was nothing but a personal matter, certainly nothing to do with the Sarge or his mission. Just as he was about to pull away, he saw the reason for the fight. A beautiful, buxom girl in *lederhosen* ran out from behind a bush and hugged the smaller man, covering his face with grateful kisses. As the bigger man writhed on the grass, the happy couple looked up at Jack and waved a thanks. He grinned and waved back, swinging the chopper back up into his surveillance pattern.

It was nice to see the good guys win sometimes, he grinned.

Which was exactly why an ex-contract pilot for the Mafia was out combing the hills and valleys of southern Germany with a map and a radio receiver tuned to a highly refined frequency, sent out by a tiny transmitter designed and built by one Herman "Gadgets" Schwarz, the resident Thomas Alva Edison of Stony Man Farm.

Grimaldi had been following the transmission since Bolan had activated it inside the Saab. Jack had kept the chopper at its maximum distance of eight kilometers so as not to tip off Bolan's new buddies.... But he had lost them somewhere here in the mountains.

A powerful jamming signal had cut him off completely.

"Stay hard, Sarge," Grimaldi had said aloud. "But stay alive."

Then a faint but distant beep-beep sounded in his headphones. He maneuvered the chopper until he found the strongest signal.

The doctor finds the pulse, he thought happily. And so he manhandled the throttle for maximum speed.

10

Bolan did not move. Not an inch. Not a breath. He kept his hands in plain sight and studied Thomas Morganslicht's shouting, contorted face. Nope, he'd never met this man before; a quick sortie through his photographic memory had revealed that much and no more.

So the big guy stayed cool, looked appropriately confused, waited for an explanation of why that 9mm Luger was waving menacingly in his face.

"Thomas!" Tanya snapped, stepping toward him. *"Was ist loss hier?"*

"Yeah, buddy," Bolan asked. "What *is* the matter?"

Thomas Morganslicht looked at the two dozen or so of his faithful who had gathered around to investigate his hollering, and he could see the mixture of curiosity and doubt in their bovine expressions. He knew that the amount of their loyalty was based on the sum of their collective experiences of fear, and therefore he aimed to unsettle them all with a shrill threat or two in the direction of the American.

Thomas holstered his Luger and laughed. It sounded like a stick scraping cement. "Just a little test of courage, Sergeant Grendal," he said, wiping the chill sweat from his forehead. "Like you have in your American universities. Fraternity, uh—" He turned to his sister. *"Wie heist das?"*

"Initiation."

"Ja. Initiation." He smiled.

Tanya looked at her brother with concern, but forced a hearty laugh. Several of the gathered group chuckled amiably and began to disperse.

Rudi the bear did neither. He had been staring at Bolan with something more than contempt, perhaps even more than hate. Occasionally one of his thick cracked lips would curl up into a half-snarl, displaying his repulsive teeth and gums. He tapped the hunk of wood methodically against his leg.

Bolan glanced around the hardsite as if he were taking in some charming scenery. By the time his eyes had swung back to the front porch of Thomas's cabin, he had estimated the personnel strength at about thirty, mostly armed with East German copies of the Soviet Makarov pistol. He had also determined that the hostages were being held in the locked garage a few cabins down, where two armed men stood guard. He had also noted the dried blood on the end of Rudi's log.

"Perhaps we should step inside?" Tanya urged her brother. "We have much to discuss."

"Yes, of course. But first, Rudi must search you, Sergeant Grendal. It is merely a, uh—"

"Formality?" Bolan offered.

"Right. A formality."

"This better be a hell of a fraternity." Bolan leaned up against the wall of the cabin as Rudi frisked him roughly, occasionally using the wood club to prod.

Bolan endured the search for concealed weapons silently. He had planted Gadgets's transmitter within the Saab, rather than on his person. He would need that transmitter. It was Grimaldi's means for locating the scene of action in order to pick up the hostages.

Rudi finished up his search and gave Bolan one last prod with his log. "Just this," he growled, tossing the Beretta to Thomas.

"Clean of heart, pure of spirit," Bolan laughed, turning around. He smiled at Thomas and Tanya in turn, but let his smile rest on Rudi for a few extra seconds.

In those seconds, although his expression did

not change, Bolan conveyed a silent message, a promise of things to come.

The driver, Hans, came out of one of the cabins, a mug of steaming coffee cupped in both hands. *"Was noch?"* he asked Thomas.

"Unload the weapon and drive the car to Munich. Wait there for further instructions."

Thomas then opened the cabin door and waved Bolan in. "Shall we, Sergeant Grendal?"

Bolan entered the cabin without looking back at the car. Within a few minutes the transmitter would be on its way to Munich, with Jack Grimaldi following close behind, pursuing a signal and waiting for a coded message.

Well, yeah, the Executioner had been alone before. Maybe he preferred it that way.

11

Jack Grimaldi flew the chopper with one eye on the sky and one on the maps spread out next to him. He had not eaten since yesterday afternoon, and was only now paying attention to the grumbling sounds of his stomach.

"Easy does it," he said to his stomach. "Dr. Grimaldi has a nice big dose of sauerbraten waiting for you. Just a few more miles."

He had followed the signal for almost thirty kilometers now, and there was no doubt where it was heading. The driving was slow and steady. Not like on the way down from Frankfurt, when the car had rocketed along the Autobahn at 150 kph. No, this driver was in no hurry, he had no major drive ahead.

Grimaldi nodded his head and smiled. In a few minutes he would be able to set his baby-bug down and phone in the target area. Within an hour the hotspot would be pinpointed and surrounded with ground support. Grimaldi would be at his receiver and waiting for the final countdown from Striker.

Yeah, within an hour, all their forces would be concentrated on the car's destination.

Munich.

12

"Just what have you heard about us?" Thomas asked.

"That you're the slimiest group of killers on three continents," Bolan said.

Rudi lurched forward, gripping his log, but Thomas held him back with a laugh. "Ha, within the next two days we should improve upon that image, eh, Rudi? Tanya? Ha!"

Bolan yawned. "Everyone should have a goal, I guess."

"And what is your goal, Sergeant Grendal?" asked Thomas.

"Money," Tanya answered for him. There was contempt in her voice.

"You have no strong political loyalties. Ideologies?" persisted her brother.

"Just one," said Bolan. "Don't give credit." Just give blame, he might have said, in this world of terror where blame is hushed by fear.

"Admirable," Tanya sneered.

Thomas flopped back on his unmade cot and

propped his head against the rough wooden wall. Tanya sat on a large tree stump that served as a stool near the fireplace. Rudi leaned his three-hundred-plus against the front door like a thick slab of iron.

Bolan went over to the canteen on the wooden table, unscrewed the cap, wiped the opening, took a long tug of water. Then he screwed the cap back on and said to Thomas, "Hope you don't mind?"

Thomas shook his head.

It was uncanny how much Tanya and Thomas looked alike. Sure, they had the same black hair that came to a dagger's point over their forehead. But there was more to it than that. They moved alike, with the same graceful yet deadly intent, as if they were always sneaking up on something. But there were differences too, particularly in the eyes. Tanya's were calm and cold, with only a minimal sign of emotion. She intellectualized everything, categorized it, dealt with it purely logically. Not so Thomas. Though his eyes were the same pale blue as his sister's, the whites were different. Little thin veins like jagged red lightning bolts shot from the corners of them toward the pupils. Bloodshot, like an alcoholic's. Although he seemed to maintain a cool exterior, something ominous was bubbling beneath his surface: and just barely beneath.

"So let's quit doing the goosestep and get down to business," Bolan suggested.

Thomas Morganslicht smiled, without humor in his eyes.

"The point, Sergeant Grendal, is that my friends and I had a tightly knit organization until you came along and disposed of Klaus."

Rudi's lips curled into a snarl.

"Oh, don't mind Rudi here," said Thomas. "He and Klaus were friends and Rudi does not make friends easily."

"He doesn't look like he could make his bed easily."

"I'm afraid Rudi does not much like you," advised Tanya.

"I'm crushed."

"You might be," Tanya added, "if Rudi ever got his hands on you."

"Look," Bolan said, "I'd like to help you guys out. I could use the business. So give me a thousand marks for that H & K that I brought here and I'll be on my way. A ride would be appreciated."

Thomas held up his hand. "Tanya also tells me you are an expert with weapons."

"I know my business."

Thomas pulled out his Luger and pointed it at Bolan. "What do you know about this?"

"Just three things. It's a 9mm Luger. It's one

of the newer versions that the Mauser Jagdwaffen factory began producing in 1971. And I'm getting real tired of looking down its barrel.''

Bolan turned for the door. Things were clearly not going well. He still did not know why they had kidnapped the athletes.

Rudi leered unpleasantly as Bolan approached him. Suddenly Bolan asked:

"How much?"

Tanya looked up surprised. "How much what?"

"How much is my percentage if I arrange for all of the weapons you want?"

"I thought you—"

"I have a source, okay? It's not a straight buy, you're going to have to take them, but they're the best you can get. Galil SAR short automatic rifles, effective up to five hundred meters with caliber five point five-six millimeters NATO. The Israelis make them with wire cutters in the bipods and bottle openers on the butt. They also have a new shipment of nine millimeter Parabellum Mini Uzis with twelve-fifty rpms.''

Thomas sat up off the cot. "How many?" he said coolly.

"Enough to outfit this little group."

"Where are they?" he said. "Who do we take them from?"

"Well, now," Bolan said with a grin. "That's the part you aren't going to like."

No, they were not going to like it one bit.

But the Executioner was counting on their need. If he counted wrong, then there was no hope for the hostages.

13

"You must be insane!"

Bolan smiled. "That depends on how badly you want those weapons."

"You're suggesting we steal them from our own people."

"Black Sunday is not your own people. Even Arafat has disassociated himself from them. In fact, word is that the faction of Black Sunday headed by Abu Sata is out to overthrow Arafat."

Bolan sat confidently on the edge of the wooden table, hunched slightly, taking another swig from the canteen. "I have some poker buddies at military intelligence who told me that a whole new shipment of these weapons was delivered last month to the Black Sunday faction in Mannheim."

"And what does your military intelligence plan to do about it?"

"What they always do," Bolan shrugged. "Nothing. Strictly wait-and-see. But you and your outfit here, you're different...."

"But they are our own people," Thomas persisted. "Politically, philosophically we are aligned, despite petty internal squabbles."

Bolan smiled. "Like I said, it all depends on how badly you need the guns. You come crying to me for guns and I come up with a reasonable solution. Now either go for it or cut bait and kiss this big-deal mission of yours goodbye."

Thomas Morganslicht paced beside his cot, nibbling on his thumbnail. When he spoke his voice was soft and distant, as if he were speaking only to himself. "Visibility, that's the key. Achieved only through reputation and recognition. Why is that so important?" He looked up suddenly, stared at Bolan and smiled. "Tell me, Sergeant Grendal, why is recognition so important for us? Is it to convey our ideals? Huh?

"Let me tell you about reputation, Sergeant, and its purposes." Thomas started pacing again, chewing harder on his fingernails. "Let me fill you in on the practicalities of running an underground liberation effort. We need money for food, lodging, clothing. Believe it or not, we purchase socks and underwear from time to time. Also medical services. As well as weapons."

"Thomas," Tanya interrupted, displeased that her brother should speak so openly with an outsider.

He waved a dismissing hand. "How do we get that money, Sergeant? Usually we steal it, robbing banks or homes or kidnapping for ransom. Sometimes those petty crimes are even riskier than our political, uh, adventures. And yet we look around at our revolutionary brothers in the Red Brigades, Japanese Red Army, IRA, PLO—"

"Black Sunday," Bolan added.

"Yes," he nodded, "especially Black Sunday. We see how they get the best equipment, plenty of operating money, all supplied by our Soviet comrades and Arab brothers, funneled and laundered through various front organizations." As his voice rose higher, the muscles in his neck began to bulge. "And we, the Zwilling Horde, though we fight for the same end, have to continue to rob banks just to eat."

"Then I don't see where you have any choice," insisted Mack Bolan. "Either you raid the Black Sunday gang in Mannheim and steal their weapons, or you postpone your coming action."

"It cannot be postponed," spat Thomas, at the peak of his intensity. "This is our only chance at it. After two days it will be too late. Rudi," he said. "Take the sergeant and throw him in with the others."

"My proposition?" Bolan asked. "And my percentage?"

"We will consider it," Tanya said. "We'll let you know."

"Just remember who is familiar with these weapons," Bolan hammered on. "Your men will need crash training before they can use any of the dandies I've been talking about."

Rudi's massive hand wrapped around Bolan's arm and jerked him toward the door. Bolan offered no resistance, allowing himself to be ushered out of the cabin while the twins of terror deliberated on his plan.

It was crazy again, sure—engineering a raid by one group of terrorists against another. But right now it was the best hope he had. Were the Morganslichts ambitious enough to do it? And would they be able to rationalize it with some slick political double-talk?

If the answer was yes, then they would need Bolan and he would have a chance of completing his mission.

If the answer was no, all bets were off.

14

"Did Grimaldi give any indication as to where the car's owner might be located?" asked a weary Brognola.

"None," said April Rose. "He and some of General Wilson's men tracked the transmitter to a blue Saab abandoned in downtown Munich. There's already a police report showing the car was stolen in Frankfurt. So that lead is dead."

Hal moved over to the computer terminal and stared at the blank screen. "Can't this damn thing tell us anything?"

"Not yet." April followed him to the screen. "Jack thinks that Mack is still near the Alps someplace, probably in the foothills. That's where Jack first encountered the jamming device. It wasn't until the car drove out of the jammer's range that he picked up its signal again."

"So we've lost him. Completely. Striker is totally on his own."

She gave a sharp look. "He's been there before."

"What about Grimaldi? Should he go back to take another look-see? Mosey around?"

"Negative, according to Jack. He doesn't want to blow Mack's cover. He's just going to sit tight in Munich and do what we're going to do. Wait. And hope."

It was a new role for Mack, no doubt at all. A new game, a new gun or two, a new kind of death—death on foreign soil with no backup of any kind. New, every which way you looked at it. He'd been there before, but not like this.

The uncertainty actually stimulated Stony Man's head fed. Striker could cope with anything that Europe could throw at him. Hal knew that for a fact.

The German terrorist philosophy was a *situational* one. Tactics and targets changed according to the fall of the chips. Modern Europe went for that kind of moral relativity, had done since the sixties. And Bolan was a master of the situational response. He had damned near invented it.

The new Colonel John Phoenix, disguised as a morally awash U.S. Army colonel stationed in Germany, was the ultimate quick-change artist of all time. Hal had no doubts whatsoever. Inside it all, Bolan would always be Bolan.

15

When Rudi swung open the garage's side door, a long spear of sunlight sliced through the dark room that caused its occupants to wince from sudden brightness.

He shoved Mack Bolan through the doorway.

A naked light bulb dangled in the middle of the dark room, casting a dim shadowy light, maybe 40 watts at most. But the small group of prisoners huddled around that pale light as if it were a blazing fire.

"Be good," Rudi said in a thick German accent, punctuating the threat by whomping his log into the wall of the garage. The room echoed with a loud thump. He laughed again and left the room. Bolan could hear the heavy iron bolt sliding into place on the other side of the door.

Within a few seconds Bolan had identified all four of his fellow occupants.

"Are you all right?" asked Babette Pavlovski, the Czech gymnast. She took a few hesitant steps closer, but stopped at the edge of the bulb's curtain of light like someone at the edge of a dark and forbidden forest.

"Yeah. Thanks. How about you folks?"

Bolan studied her. She was tall for a gymnast, nearly six feet, but all of it looked solid sinew. Her thin blond hair was pulled back into a tight bun, making her look older than the thirty years he guessed her to be. She wore a maroon running suit with white piping up the legs and sleeves; the suit was smudged with dirt and grime. He noted how she moved with an animal's ease, as if she were in complete control of every muscle in her body.

"You must forgive the accommodations," she said ironically, "but our hosts are less than considerate." She pointed to a dark corner of the room where Bolan could barely make out the form of a small squat object. "That's the toilet. A plastic bucket with no lid. We share it. But don't worry, they empty it once a day."

A tall muscular young man with curly brown hair and a bushy mustache took a step toward Bolan. His voice was angry and mixed with fear. Bolan recognized him as Udo Ganz, the German skier who had captured two golds in the Olympics six years before. "What are you?" Udo asked with a halting German accent.

"A sergeant in the United States Army."

"No, no," he shook his head impatiently. "Your sport. What is your sport?"

A short, thin Oriental man stepped directly beneath the hanging light bulb. He wore jeans and a black turtleneck sweater. Above his lip was a pencil-thin slash of a mustache. Bolan could have recognized him without having been warned of his kidnapping: Mako Samata's martial arts studios were advertised all over Europe. "There is no practical use for football skills here," he said in a French accent, making the immediate assumption of Bolan's elective recreation.

"What do you mean, practical use?" Bolan asked. "What use do they have for you?"

The martial arts master released a sardonic laugh. "You will see soon enough, my friend."

"Don't mind him," Babette sighed. "He likes to play the inscrutable Oriental. Too many Charlie Chan movies."

Bolan looked past the three of them at the burly man hunkered down on his heels, hugging his knees. He was just beyond the light, his face partially obscured. "What about him?" Bolan pointed.

"That's Clifford Barnes-Fenwick, the Welsh archer. A silver and a bronze." She lowered her voice. "Used to do trick shooting for a while."

At that the silent man looked up and Bolan

could see his haggard face. And the softball-size knob over his right eye. The bruise surrounding it was a nasty purple-yellow-black. But even worse was the nose, which looked as if it had been slammed by a locomotive. Most of it was pushed to one side at an impossible angle. Crusted blood clung to the edges. The injuries made it difficult to judge, but Bolan figured him to be near fifty, easily the oldest of the group.

"What happened to you?" Bolan asked him.

The big Welshman stared at Bolan a few seconds, then lowered his head back to his knees.

"That fat gorilla did it," Babette explained. "Cliff wouldn't do what they asked, so Rudi clubbed him with the log. You've seen the log?"

"What is it that they want you to do?" Bolan persisted.

"Well—"

"Hold it!" Udo Ganz interrupted. "We don't know anything about this man. He could be bad news."

The leggy blonde raised her eyebrows. "What, a spy, Udo? For what purpose?"

Bolan cut in. "Maybe some introductions are in order. Then we can fill each other in on what the hell is going on around here. I'm Sergeant Edsel Grendal."

The others formally introduced themselves in

turn, all except the Welsh archer who remained huddled at the edge of the light. Each recounted the details of their kidnapping experience. Except Bolan.

He asked one more time, "What exactly do they want from you?"

"Knowledge," Mako said, his hands erupting in a series of expert lightning slashes.

"That's what we think, anyway," Babette qualified.

"Explain."

"All they make us do every day is to practice routines while they all stand around and watch. Mako here has to do a sneaking through the woods routine, surprising two guards and disabling them for real with a couple of his fancy chops."

In the few moments he had been in the tiny garage, Bolan had noticed the icy teeth of the cold nipping at his skin. The temperature could be no more than a few degrees above freezing in this dark hovel. "How do they expect you to survive here. . .?" he asked.

"They don't!" Udo barked, desperation in his voice. Bolan noted the man's creeping hysteria and filed away the information.

"They don't keep us in here all the time," the lady gymnast said. "We're only locked up when we aren't practicing. At night they allow us to sleep in a preheated cabin. By then the exercise and cold have worn us down—even if we could escape, we wouldn't have the energy to go anywhere."

"Some of us, anyway," Mako said quietly.

The accusation hung tensely in the air. Udo's eyes widened with sudden anger. Then he pivoted away, turning his back to the three of them.

Bolan realized that unless they were rescued quickly, the abducted athletes might destroy each other—and, forever, their chances for survival. "What do they make *you* practice, Babette?" he asked.

"The balance beam. Nothing tricky, just running as fast as I can along a four-inch by twenty-foot wall that they have constructed. All I do is run back and forth along the edge, carrying a knapsack containing two bricks. Not terribly difficult."

"Maybe not for you," Bolan commented. "What do the others do?"

"Udo here skis a rather steep slope, carrying the same kind of knapsack with two bricks that I carry."

"It's a little more complicated than that," Udo interrupted, turning back to face them. "Not only must I navigate the steep slope, but I must also make a twenty-foot jump off a hidden ramp. Then, while I'm in midair, I must drop the sack into the back of a truck that drives under me.''

"Sounds difficult," Bolan said.

Babette smiled. ''Not for one of the best skiers in the world.''

Udo Ganz shrugged modestly, obviously pleased. "At one time, maybe. But now...?'' He shrugged again.

"What about your silent friend?" Bolan nodded at Clifford Barnes-Fenwick, squatting several feet away from the others, still hugging his knees.

"They want him to practice a series of unusual archery shots. One from two hundred yards, and another in which he must fire off five bull's-eyes from thirty yards, but all within fifteen seconds.''

"Sounds impossible. Is that why he refuses?''

Babette lowered her voice again, more out of respect than any possibility that he could not hear her. "No, Cliff can do the shots all right. But he retired last year from his trick-shooting career following, well, an accident. His fourteen-year-old son was killed. It wasn't Cliff's fault, he'd been away on tour. But his son and some friends were practicing tricks they had seen him do, and one of them accidentally shot an arrow into Cliff's son. After that, he quit his job and refused to pick up a bow again.

These people have beaten him, but they don't want to hurt him to the point where he won't be able to shoot."

"I've got a feeling they may not be so careful next time." Bolan moved directly under the hanging bulb. He motioned the others to come closer. All except Clifford obliged.

"I can't go into details yet," he told them. "But I can guarantee that you'll soon have a chance to escape. What you make of that chance will be up to you."

"When does this 'chance' take place," Mako asked, the skepticism thick in his voice.

"Sometime over the next two days. That's the best I can do."

"Who are you?" Udo asked. "Army Intelligence?"

"Just a guy in the same tight spot that you're in. Now, you're going to hear me saying some things and see me doing some things that won't make you think I'm on your side. But I am. You have to believe that, no matter what happens. Everything depends on that. Do you understand?"

Before they could respond, the door was wrenched open and Rudi's mountainous frame stood in the doorway. Bright sunlight streaked around his body like white flames. He stepped into the room, tapping his log into his open palm.

Tanya Morganslicht appeared behind him, her expression calm, her voice crisp and businesslike.

"We have decided to exploit you, Sergeant," she said to Bolan. "Welcome to the Zwilling Horde."

"What exactly is my percentage of this deal?" Bolan asked immediately. "In dollars and cents."

Tanya allowed herself a small smile. "You have just come within an inch of horrible death, and all you can think about is your percentage. You amaze even me."

Bolan started toward the open door, but before he had taken a full step, Babette grabbed his arm and whirled him around. She slapped his face with stinging authority.

"You lying traitor!" she spat.

Tanya laughed. "Well, Sergeant Grendal, apparently your charms have their limitations after all."

"Yeah," Bolan said, rubbing his cheek. "Apparently."

16

Bolan sat in the back of the VW van with six other members of the assault team as they sped through the cool German night. The big Heckler & Koch G-11 lay flat across his knees like a streamlined hunk of modern sculpture. Tanya Morganslicht was driving, and was also holding onto the H & K's ammo clips until this tense party had reached the Black Sunday hideout.

Rudi literally rode shotgun, the thick log temporarily replaced by a Stevens Model No. 77 12-gauge shotgun with slide-action and side ejection. It had only a five-shot tubular magazine, but each of those five shots was like a shower of flaming meteors. Every mile or so, Rudi would look over his shoulder at Bolan. Through the back window of the van, Bolan could see Thomas Morganslicht's duplicate van as it tagged close behind with an additional six armed terrorists. It was a small force, but if Hal's monthly update briefing had been correct, it was sufficient to handle the slightly larger Black Sunday group.

Bolan leaned his head against the metal side of the van, let the rhythmic vibrations massage the back of his scalp.

"Cigarette?" one of the hardmen asked the soldier sitting next to Bolan. The young terrorist patted his pockets and shrugged.

Bolan reached into his pocket and pulled out a pack of the brand he had seen in the dead Sergeant Grendal's pocket. "Here, pal," he said.

"Ah, American!" the terrorist nodded appreciatively.

"Pass 'em around," Bolan said, tossing him the pack.

There was a murmur of pleasure and thanks from the six as they all reached for a cigarette.

Bolan replayed the scene in the garage. He had calmly urged the hostaged athletes to be ready for an escape, but Mako had been skeptical. The Welsh archer had ignored him. Udo Ganz was so shaky he could not be relied on. And the only one who had originally trusted him had slapped his face when Tanya Morganslicht announced his introduction into the Horde. Of course he had warned them that they would hear some things that would make them doubt him. Maybe he hadn't been convincing enough. It was hard to move into a group of desperate people and gain their trust. But if he failed, it would be impossible to get them moving when the time was right. They either had faith or they did not. If they did not, there would be no escape for them.

What were the opportunities opening up for him on this mission now? Killing Tanya and Thomas at a premature moment would not solve things at all. They might be the brains of this vicious, crazy group, but once they were gone their followers would scatter to other berserk groups, and perhaps carry the Plan with them, whatever it was. Bolan wanted the big kill, he knew that now.

Tanya Morganslicht brought the van to a halt. They were parked on the side of a deserted road. She slid out of her seat, stooping slightly as she turned to face her men. Even in the dark, Bolan could see the face glowing with excitement at what was to come. Her hair was pulled back and pinned to the top of her head, making the sharp widow's peak look like some sort of Roman helmet.

"We must do what is necessary for our cause," she began. Bolan looked out the back of the van and saw her brother addressing his troops also, probably with the same rehearsed speech. "Even if it means some of our political brothers and sisters must die. Our struggle is larger, more important than any individual lives. We need their weapons to complete our mission, and in two days, when our allies in the East see what we have accomplished, they will understand the actions we are forced to take tonight.'' She paused and stared at each man in turn. ''Naturally, we can take no survivors to identify us. So be thorough.''

She reached around to her seat, turned and tossed two clips for the H & K to Bolan. He caught each, jamming the first into the gun and storing the second in his pocket.

''Thanks,'' said Bolan. How kind of her. She would never know how kind, he thought to himself. Because he was going to show his gratitude in the unique Executioner way....

17

It was a small two-story farmhouse on a deserted stretch of dirt road, just twelve kilometers beyond Mannheim. Strategically it was a strong enough hardsite, with easily defendable perimeters and plenty of unobstructed view from the farmhouse. This was not going to be easy.

A frontal assault would be suicide. The sixteen of them charging up the dusty driveway leading to the farmhouse could be picked clean by a twelve-year-old with a slingshot. Trying to bluff their way in with a broken-down-car story would not work either: these people had tried most such ploys during their own careers as terrorists.

Tanya tapped Bolan on the shoulder and pointed her gun where she wanted him to go. He nodded, cradled the H & K in the crook of his arm, and crawled on his elbows and knees through the heavy underbrush near the barbed-wire fence that circled the darkened land. Rudi had already cut an opening and most of the troops had bellied through.

It was an outrage of history that half the law enforcement agencies in the world knew all about this farmhouse, and yet did nothing. There were a lot of embarrassed mumbles about "circumstantial evidence" and such, but the real reason was that they were afraid to make arrests for fear of reprisals. No, if the law was going to take them at all they would have to kill them, outright and immediately. And that, they found themselves unable to do. Thus the place exlsted, a sitting target for the Executioner, awaiting its fate from beyond the law. Good.

Mack Bolan knew this Black Sunday group for what it was, a mindless collection of writhing vipers with no purpose but destruction and murder. They had started out as the Zwilling Horde had started, with random bombings and occasional murders. But they made their public debut with a more spectacular public crime, and were destined for even bigger publicity resulting from even greater horrors. Eventually, indeed, the publicity had been too much, altogether too negative, and the PLO's Arafat had demanded they stop. But most of these creeps could not stop, did not want to, no matter how it hurt their "cause."

Bolan looked around at either flank as a half-moon of sixteen terror soldiers advanced on the farmhouse. He appreciated the irony of his situation. As bad as the terrorists holed up inside were, these Zwilling Horde people were even crazier. And now one group was going to destroy the other. Bolan smiled a wide, honest smile. Yeah, he liked that idea.

He would have preferred to be clad in his own assault outfit, the .44 AutoMag thundermaker strapped to his side, the whispering Beretta tucked under his arm, the M-16/203 with the 40mm grenade launcher clutched to his gut. Still, this H & K was one hell of a weapon. It would have to do for now. The lunatic Thomas Morganslicht had his Beretta, and the regaining of that would be a substrategy of its own.

The advance was halfway from the vans to the farmhouse when the first shot cracked loudly through the crisp night air. It was followed by stuttering automatic fire from one of the Horde, a piercing scream, silence. Bolan saw a Black Sunday hardguy stumble forward off the farmhouse porch. So now the element of surprise was lost.

The Zwilling Horde opened fire on the farmhouse. The crackle of imitation Makarov pistols sounded in the dark. The Horde was pinned down by automatic fire with still thirty bullet-riddled yards to cover.

Bolan spotted Tanya across the field to his left and crouched toward her, bullets kicking up dirt clods, nipping at his heels. He dived the last ten feet.

"I told you to hold your position for the cross fire," she uttered angrily. "Disobeying orders is punishable by death, Sergeant."

She lifted her rifle to her shoulder and once more took aim at the farmhouse. She pumped round after round at the old building.

Bolan ran forward, aware that at least seven other men were with him as the farmhouse was sprayed with repeating rounds. After covering ten yards, these men dropped for cover and began firing as the next seven soldiers came up over the same ground.

One of the seven that had run with Bolan had caught a slug in the forehead and lay sprawled five feet from the second wave of soldiers and ten feet from the top of his head. Two more men were picked off in the second wave.

Tanya Morganslicht dropped to her chest next to Bolan as he continued to fire the H & K at the nearest farmhouse window. The increased volume of shouting in the farmhouse indicated the terminal nervousness in there.

Bolan led the next charge, gaining ten more yards but bloodily losing another man. Tanya led her own group through the hell of bullets, and she also lost a man, with another wounded in the groin.

The last run cost them two more soldiers, but now they were pressed against the solid farmhouse walls. They were safe here, as long as they kept away from the windows.

And then the Black Sunday hardguys burst through the front and back doors simultaneously, spilling six or seven troops from each exit into the smoke-filled night. They were all armed with new Uzi machine guns, and they knew how to use them. But they were at the disadvantage of having to come out into the open to fire them, and the Horde was waiting with guns trained on each door. There was a fearful echo of explosions as the Horde opened fire on the rival terrorists, literally shredding their targets.

According to Tanya, Thomas and Rudi were on the other side of the building—which was just as well, because Bolan did not want to have Rudi and his shotgun behind him during this next phase.

"Und jehts?" Thomas Morganslicht yelled out from the other side of the house.

"Any suggestions?" panted the woman terrorist leader.

"Sure, but it'll cost you," answered Mack Bolan.

"How much?"

"Two men at least. And that's for sure dead, not maybe."

"Acceptable," she said without hesitation.

"Okay. We blast the doors, send a man through each, one at the front and one at the back. Once both doors are open, we chew up the survivors in a cross fire—as long as we're aware of where our own people are. Naturally the first men through each door are dog meat."

"Dog meat?"

"Dead."

"Naturally," Tanya Morganslicht said.

She waved three of her nearest men over to her, then whispered instructions and they hurried off to pass the instructions on.

"Erich," she called to one of the younger men—the one who had gotten the American cigarette from Bolan. "You will have the honor of leading us through the door."

Erich tried to smile to acknowledge the honor. But it was a sick smile, full of the knowledge of death.

"Don't worry, Erich," she said in a soothing voice, "we will cover you."

He tried to speak but only choked on the words. Instead he just nodded. Then, suddenly, he was running across the porch toward the front door, his Uzi blasting away at the lock.

Bolan could hear the same commotion coming from the other side of the building as another kamikaze "volunteer" charged the back door.

Bolan gripped the H & K tightly in his fists, and hunched into a ready position.

Erich's concentrated fire on the lock caused the door to swing open, but that was all that Erich would get to see of the inside. A flurry of automatic fire punched through the space and continued on into Erich's face, spraying blood and wet clots of brain and chips of skull over his waiting comrades.

"Go!" Tanya screamed, and her followers opened fire on the doorway until everything that surrounded it was nothing more than a mass of splinters and sawdust. There were screams of pain from inside and the sound of footsteps clambering up wooden stairs.

"Go!" she hollered again and her three remaining troops piled through the front door, their Uzis chattering diatribes of death. When the last of her men had made it through the door, Tanya followed with her own captured Uzi blazing from chest level.

Bolan was happy to let the kills continue.

He heard a second-story window being opened. He ducked into the recess of the front door, his back pressed against the wall so that those above could not see him.

It wasn't much more than a fifteen-foot drop, and the first two made it with no problem. Someone from above tossed their Uzis to them, then they waved for the third person to follow. She did. But when she hit the ground, Bolan could hear her ankle snap with a crack. She muffled her scream so as not to warn the attackers inside, but it was obvious she would not be able to walk.

The two men exchanged looks, then glanced back at her. She was apparently pleading for them to take her with them, but the two men had already made up their minds. They could not make it with her dragging them down, nor could they risk leaving her behind to scream a warning.

But nor did they want to alert the troops inside where they were, so they could not shoot. So while the girl continued her whispered pleading, the taller man assured her that they would help. As his comrade soothed her, the second man drove the butt of his gun into the side of her head, crushing her skull.

It was not a blow meant to stun or knock out. It was meant to kill, and from the way she toppled backward like a bludgeoned steer, Bolan knew it had done its job. The men started to run.

"Hold it," Bolan said softly. The menace in his voice found their ears despite the loud carnage inside the house.

The two hardguys brought their Uzis up as they pivoted in a low crouch, but Bolan was already firing, stitching a row of wet red buttons across their chests. He zigzagged another row from head to crotch for each, spinning them around before they collapsed.

Inside, it was a bloody mess, with weapons and shredded flesh splattered across the walls. Bolan was careful where he walked because the thick pools of blood made the floor slippery.

"This one's still alive," Thomas Morganslicht said, pointing at one sprawled man, his eyes half-open, blood foaming at his mouth.

Rudi stepped carelessly over a few bodies and stood next to the man Thomas had pointed out. Then with a mighty cry he lifted his right leg knee-high into the air and stomped down on the man's throat with his heavy boot. The body jerked a few times then remained still. Rudi looked over at Bolan and smiled.

"The rest are dead," Tanya proclaimed as she finished her tour. "That takes care of witnesses. Now let's load the weapons."

Bolan counted eight remaining of the Zwilling

Horde, including himself. There were at least
twenty-five dead among the Black Sunday
group, so it had been a successful raid in terms
of objectives. However, they had lost eight of
their troops. There were more back at the camp,
of course. . .enough for the big operation to
come?

Bolan would find that one out soon enough.

18

"Let's kill him now," Thomas Morganslicht said, collapsing onto his cot with a deep sigh.

"In time," Tanya answered. She walked over to the stove and poured herself a cup of thick German coffee.

"We don't need him anymore. We have the weapons we need for the day after tomorrow."

"No," she said, shaking her head and blowing steam from the coffee. "We go tomorrow."

"Tomorrow? That's too soon. Everything has been planned for the next day."

"No it hasn't. It never was. I told everyone the wrong day for security reasons."

Thomas jumped up from the cot and wagged his finger angrily at his sister. "But you should have told me! I'm in command here."

"Co-command," she said icily.

He shrugged. "Well, you know what I mean."

"Yes, dear brother, I know exactly what you mean. Sometimes before you even mean it."

Thomas began pacing beside the cot. His voice was petulant but accepting, the way it always was when his sister outmaneuvered him. "Still, I should have been told."

She took a sip of coffee and smiled soothingly. "Look, Thomas, when we decided to form this little group, we agreed that I would be in charge of security. Okay, I could have told you the truth, but then you'd have had to pretend to everyone else that we were going a day later. And we both know how hard it is for you to pretend. You were never good at it when we were children, nor are you any better at it now."

"Well, I—" he protested.

"There's no need to deny it. I'm glad you're that way. Your honesty and candor is what make our troops follow you so readily into battle. They trust you. That's why you're in charge of training them."

"Yes, yes, that's true."

"Of course it is." She widened her smile until he turned away, then she threw it away like old coffee grounds. As always, she had told him what he had wanted to hear, and that would satisfy him for the time being. Poor Thomas had always been a little weak in the brain. Though he was older by 86 seconds, she always looked upon him as her younger brother. Had it not been for her, he'd have flunked out of the university and be working in a Volkswagen factory somewhere. Some people were born to follow, and some were born to lead.

But Thomas had his uses. Men still did not like taking orders from a woman. So whenever possible, she gave the orders to Thomas and by the time he had passed them on to the men, he had convinced himself that he'd made them up. It worked quite well.

"Tomorrow we take the sergeant with us on the mission," continued Tanya. "After tonight's raid we are short of men. And we can use his military experience. Despite our own experience, he is still a professional and we are amateurs."

"Why would he help us?" bleated Thomas.

She laughed dryly. "We will offer him money. And after we're successful tomorrow, you and Rudi can kill him."

Thomas smiled. "And make him an example?"

"If you must."

"It's the only way to show the world that we mean business," seethed the brother.

His sister smiled. "After tomorrow, history will know us in all our crimson magnificence. Do what you will, Thomas, do what has to be done."

19

Rudi sat on the edge of his cot, the gnarled log balanced across his knees, his meaty hands wrapped around each end. He scowled across the room at Bolan, huge teeth glistening with saliva.

"We have to stop meeting like this," Bolan grinned.

Rudi tightened his grip on the log. "American humor," he sneered and spat on the dusty floor.

"Yeah, well, you don't exactly keep me in stitches, guy. Though I think you'd like to."

"Shut up!" spluttered Rudi, saliva spraying from his lips. He struggled to control his temper. It was what the twins would want him to do, but still it was so difficult at times, especially with this infuriating American. There was something about this man that made Rudi seriously nervous. Rudi had, to his knowledge, never been afraid of anything before in his life.

But with this American it was different. The

U.S. Army sergeant goaded and pushed in such a way that Rudi wanted to crush him. Breaking his back would not be enough, he would have to use his thumbs to gouge out those taunting eyes, too. He hated those eyes. They were hard confident eyes that somehow drained Rudi of his own confidence. And that could not be tolerated. He would try to control his temper, for the sake of the twins, but there were limits beyond which even he could not be pushed.

"Enough talk," Rudi warned. "You talk too much, but say nothing."

"An American custom," Bolan nodded. "We call it small talk. It's supposed to make us good buddies."

"Buddies, hah!" Rudi snorted and spat on the floor.

"Is it true what they say about you?"

The muscles in Rudi's neck bulged like steel cables on a bridge. "What do they say?"

"That the difference between you and an ape is that the ape smells better."

Three hundred pounds of screaming flesh came hurtling across the small cabin, all of it aimed at Mack Bolan.

The Executioner dived to one side. Rudi went crashing into the cot, smashing it to splinters.

He arose like a maddened bull and lunged at

his quarry, grabbing a new hunk of wood in his hand as he did so.

Bolan grabbed the man-mountain by the face, slowing his advance, and held back the club with all the strength of his left arm.

Then he smashed his forehead into the thick wide nose of the giant terrorist. Rudi's cartilage cracked dully and a sticky spray of warm blood shot out of his nostrils as if from a garden hose.

Rudi cried out, and Bolan snapped his head forward again, even harder. Rudi wailed and his grip loosened in every way. Rudi had had enough. He stood with his frying-pan hands covering his splintered nose and badly bloodied face, gulping air greedily through his mouth.

But Bolan was just beginning.

He kicked the beast in the stomach. His lightning-fast right combat boot was propelled by a steel-spring complex of thigh and calf muscles that had the power to smash bricks and disintegrate doors.

The impact was the equivalent of a motor being thrown at human flesh. When the force connected with Rudi, it blasted the wind out of him, but he did not crumble.

Fine, thought Bolan. He wants humiliation and that is what he will get. Rudi's rage and shame will be my ally—it will turn against him and will destroy him.

Bolan's next kick was higher, connecting with the chest.

A blood-soaked Rudi, his sinuses open to the wind, grabbed the foot immediately, even as it sank into his gross pectorals like a cannonball into a listing ship.

He twisted the ankle in his grasp until Bolan was tossed over and facing the floor, head down, only his hands keeping his nose from being ground into the filth of the hovel floor. Rudi was dangling Mack Bolan upside down like some empty wheelbarrow.

Bolan grabbed the vile creature's knees and took aim for his next shot.

With the swiftness of a karate chop, he brought his head up with a jerk, aiming for the frontal pelvic bone, punching his speeding cranium into the German's upper crotch with all the Zen overkill of one whose aim goes far beyond the actual target.

This effect was to bend Rudi over into a forward roll as his testicles continued on their new journey back up the bladder into a cave of endless pain. He exhaled hideously as his body tumbled toward the floor, Bolan rolling with him to come upright as Rudi groveled.

Bolan was grinning. His head had now

bounced three times off of bone, and each time the damage was so much greater than the impact might indicate. The nose hits had completely screwed up the workings of the bloated terrorist's face, meanwhile sending shudders of shock and pain waves of splinter-scrape all through the crazed Aryan's skull, as blood and mucous slime spewed forth unchecked from the facial wreckage. Then the pelvic shot had sent spasms through the beast's scrotum so severe that the solar plexus itself had gone numb with airless apoplexy. Rudi's fat viscera convulsed inside him.

The Executioner's smile was not one of pleasure, nor amusement. It was a bitter one, adopted only to restrain his flaring anger. It was a smile of menace, repressing like a pressurized mask the thunderclap fury that could explode at any time.

Mack Bolan once more sent a foot flying into the body of Rudi, now lying doubled-over on the floor. The kick connected with Rudi's thick throat. Groaning turned to a bubbling choke.

"That one's for Munich," intoned the Executioner.

Another vicious kick found its home on the carcass of the writhing giant.

"That one's for Mountbatten."

Yet another kick buried Bolan's foot deep into Rudi's quivering flesh. The blows were a litany for the victim of terrorist outrages. If the victims could not fight back, the Executioner would do it for them. As he lashed out at Rudi to humiliate him, to shame him—solely to set him up for the plans he had for Rudi in his unfolding strategy—the Executioner became grievously saddened. It hurt him to invoke the names of the dead and the maimed, the more so because of society's shameful reluctance to avenge their suffering.

Why does modern mankind allow the gutless warfare of terrorism to continue while the host countries whimper their toothless statements of official frowning? Why does the language itself betray basic decency, so that terrorists are said by newsreaders to have taken "responsibility" instead of "blame" for their cowardly and disgusting acts?

Why don't we call it as it is?

"And that one's for the children." The last kick was to the kidney, its quick agility and direct force communicating very powerfully Mack Bolan's position as regards the murder and the maiming of young kids who—in their hundreds now—strayed innocently into the death zone of maniacs.

It was then that Bolan saw the door ajar.

Tanya Morganslicht stood in the doorway, her hands on her hips, lips curled in cruel amusement. "It pleases me that you two have found some way to pass the time."

Rudi struggled to rise. He was in panic now and wheezed painfully as he breathed against the bruises that were luridly discoloring his upper body.

"He forced me," Rudi gasped. He was standing now, but bent over from the white pain that was twisting into his groin. "He tried to escape...I stopped him," he burbled in phlegm-soaked German.

"Yes, so I see." She stooped over and picked up his club, handing it to him. "After you have cleaned yourself, pass the command among the men that there has been a change in plan. We proceed with our planned attack tomorrow. There will be a final run through in the morning and everyone had better do magnificently." Her voice crackled with electricity.

Rudi left in agony. Tanya closed the door behind him. "I told you he didn't like you," she said.

"I've always had trouble making friends," Bolan said. "Maybe I'm just too shy."

She shook her head. "Somehow I doubt that, Sergeant. Relax, please."

"It's why I joined the army, to meet people..."

"Your lack of political commitment is disgusting," she said. "Sit down while I talk."

The woman let her eyes roam over Bolan's face and body. "You remind me so much of my father. A fine man, well-liked in the community, an architect. Respected by everyone. He gave to charities, particularly a Zionist group in our town. My own father, donating large amounts of money for the theft of Palestine! We often asked him why he did it, my brother and I."

She continued to gaze at Bolan's glistening neck and chest, but there was a faraway look in her eyes that indicated she was lost in her personal history.

"Then one day at the university, Thomas and I were approached by PLO recruiters. They were aware of our sentiments concerning Israel and the Zionists. And they showed us why our father was so 'dedicated' to the Zionist cause. As an architect during the war, he had personally designed two concentration camps."

Mack Bolan was still catching his breath from his recent exertion. Tanya searched his face for a reaction. When he offered her none she continued. "It was such a freeing experience, that information. Now we felt free to be who we really were, to follow our own beliefs and let our father wallow in his guilt and self-pity with the hoodlum Jews." Her cheeks were flushed with emotion. "It wasn't too long after that that Thomas and I traveled to Libya for a summer's combat training in revolutionary methods."

"Terrorism," muttered a hard Mack Bolan.

She shrugged. "It doesn't matter what you call it. When we win, we'll be called revolutionary heroes. Until then, we'll be called terrorists."

She unfastened the tight combat bun of her hair and shook it free. The shiny black mane splashed like dark waves over her shoulders. She walked slowly to the fireplace, removed the hurricane lamp from the mantel, tilted the glass bell and lit the wick, then placed the lamp on the table in the center of the room. She switched off the overhead light.

"I hope you don't mind being roommates with Rudi," she said. "He's been so lonely since you killed his friend Klaus."

"What you mean is, you don't trust me and you want someone to stand guard. Especially now that tomorrow is D-Day."

Tanya ignored Bolan's words. Instead she turned to face him where he sat on the edge of his damaged cot, and she began to unbutton her blouse.

The room was semidark, washed with swaying shadows from the flickering hurricane lamp. It reminded Bolan of being at the bottom of a lighted swimming pool. He watched quietly as she unfastened each button, not hurriedly, but not with deliberate slowness either—methodically, as if she were field stripping a rifle. When she had finished with the last button of her green combat shirt, Bolan confirmed what he'd known all along, that she wore no bra despite her ample breasts.

Tanya took a few steps closer to him, as if waiting for him to make the next move. Her shirt hung open, revealing smooth dark skin and the soft swell of firm breasts. "We've decided to let you live," she said suddenly, her voice all business. "And, after completing our mission tomorrow, we will give you a percentage of the profits."

"How big a percentage?" Bolan asked.

There was an edge of anger in her voice. "Big enough. You should learn to be happy with what you get, grateful even."

Bolan let his eyes drift down to her open shirt. "And how do you want me to show this gratitude?"

"However I decide," she said, taking another step toward him.

There was the sound of a rapid knock on the door. Without waiting for a reply, Hermann pushed into the room. "Say, Rudi, I wanted to know...." He looked up, surveyed the room, lingered an extra moment on Tanya's open blouse, began stammering. "I-I, uh...Rudi was supposed...I'll j-just...." He started to back out the door.

"Idiot!" Tanya barked. "Come here!"

Hermann nervously closed the door and marched toward her. The buxom commander made no attempt to rebutton her blouse. Somehow that was even more demeaning to the German, as if his opinion was too insignificant to care about.

"Don't you know any better than to enter a cabin without being invited in?"

"Yes, but I thought Rudi was, well, I thought..."

Her hand shot through the air and slapped Hermann across the cheek. His head snapped to one side.

"I don't care what you thought. This is not Rudi's cabin. It is my cabin. *All* the cabins are *my* cabin. You are permitted to stay in one of my cabins because I choose to suffer your presence. Do you understand?"

He looked at Bolan sheepishly.

"Don't look at him," she yelled, slapping him again with both a forehand and backhand. Blood swelled on his lower lip and trickled down his chin. "Now answer me."

"Yes, Commander Morganslicht. I understand."

"Interesting training technique," Bolan said. "There's a little of the storm trooper in you after all."

Tanya spun around, her eyes black and blazing. "You think my troops aren't loyal to me because I am forced to discipline them occasionally? How little you understand us, Sergeant Grendal. It is not like your own decadent army. I am a parent to my followers, treating them as I would my own children. And sometimes, like any parent, I must punish them for their own good and that of their family."

"Yeah, sure."

"You doubt me?"

"Nope. Just wouldn't want to turn my back on them if I were you."

She walked over to the hurricane lamp and carefully removed the hot glass cover. The shadows in the room shifted slightly. "Hermann," she said and he walked over to where she stood. "Give me your left hand."

Without hesitation, he stuck out his left

hand which she guided by the fingertips until it
hovered less than two inches above the yellow
flame. Hermann winced, his face clenching
into a tight sweating mask of endurance. She
held the hand there, all the time staring into
Bolan's eyes and smiling. The sickening sweet
smell of burning flesh wafted through the air.
Bolan could hear the skin sizzling and blister-
ing.

"Enough," she said, turning the hand away
from the hungry flame.

Sweat dripped down Hermann's face, pain
knotted his brow. He stood still, without a
sound. Tanya flipped the burned hand over
and showed it to Bolan. The flesh was charred
in the center, still smoking around the crisp
circle. It looked as if a small comet had struck
his palm. "That is loyalty, Sergeant Grendal.
The type your kind will never fathom. That's
because with us, loyalty is repaid." She lifted
Hermann's damaged hand lovingly to her
mouth and kissed the blistered wound. Then
she lowered it again, slipping it under her open
blouse and pressing it against her firm breast.
Despite his intense pain Hermann stared
greedily at her open blouse.

Tanya smiled at him and patted his cheek.
"Now go get this bandaged."

He left quickly.

"Naturally I used his left hand so as not to jeopardize his fitness with a rifle for tomorrow's assault."

"How thoughtful."

She replaced the glass bell on the hurricane lamp and turned back to Bolan. "Your sarcasm does not bother me, Sergeant. I have been very good to these men. I have slept with most of them at least once. Does that shock you?"

"No, it bores me."

She stood staring at Bolan for a full minute without moving. Her face was a fixed mask etched in ice.

Bolan returned her stare without blinking. He tried to penetrate the frosty exterior to understand what went on inside her head. From observation he had determined that both the twins were certifiably crazy. Thomas Morganslicht was probably born that way, or at least acted as if he'd always been nuts. But Tanya Morganslicht seemed to have chosen craziness as a life-style. And that made her the more dangerous.

Finally she broke off her stare, though Bolan figured she could have kept it up for hours had she wanted to. She buttoned the front of her blouse and walked to the door, pausing only to say, "You will need your rest for tomorrow." Then she closed the door behind her.

As Bolan stretched out on the surviving cot he tried to formalize a plan to free the hostages, foil tomorrow's mission, and devastate the Zwilling Horde until they were nothing more than a smoking hole in the ground. Simple, sure.

The situation was an arousing one for the Executioner. Thomas Morganslicht had hated him from the start. After his humiliating beating, Rudi Blau would probably try to kill him at first opportunity. And now he had alienated Tanya Morganslicht—until tonight his only ally. Yeah, things were heating up all right. And tomorrow they would boil over. The question was, who would be scalded most?

20

General Fordham "Cruiser" Wilson tightened the belt of his bathrobe as he walked down the long staircase. It was barely 0500 but the bright morning sun was already seeping through an early fog all over Germany. He loved these crisp, clear German mornings, remembering fondly how many of their sunrises he had witnessed when he was younger. A smile spread across his face and he shook his head like a proud father at the young man he used to be. Ah, well, never again. Not with these kinds of responsibilities.

He tightened his bathrobe again and wandered through the living room into the kitchen. He was surprised to find his houseguest up already, fully dressed, shaved, sipping freshly brewed coffee while he read the morning newspaper.

"Up early, aren't you, Mr. Grimaldi?"

Jack shrugged. "Not for me."

"I see," the general said. But he knew better. He had seen the concern and worry on this man's face ever since he had returned from Munich without the remarkable Colonel Phoenix. The general was intrigued by the devotion this mysterious colonel seemed to inspire. Hell, he'd even found himself willing to follow the man's orders.

The general too had inspired men to fierce loyalty, back when he was a commander in Korea. Despite heavy casualties and biting cold, his men had followed him into the helljaws of battle after battle. That's where he'd picked up the nickname "Cruiser," because he and his men plowed through the enemy like a runaway battlecruiser. Medals, sure, and plenty of citations, but the one thing he had earned there that really mattered was his men's respect. That was all that counted.

Well, now it was time to let some of the younger men take over the fight.

"You read German?" General Wilson said, pointing at the local newspaper Grimaldi was leafing through.

"Nope, I just look at the pictures and wonder why the people in them look as dopey as the people in photos back home."

"I guess it's the nature of newspapers to capture people at their worst."

"Maybe so." Jack toyed absently with the spoon in his coffee cup.

"Look, Grimaldi," the general said, pouring himself a cup of coffee, "I don't know much about this Colonel Phoenix of yours except that he's got a top secret clearance that runs all the way to the White House. And I know a couple other things about him that I didn't get from any report."

"Yeah, what's that?"

"I know from the way he handled Sergeant Grendal that he's a tough man. I know from the way he staged that fake shoot-out here that he's a smart man. And I know from those reports about the Zwilling Horde massacre of the Black Sunday group that he's got them running in circles chasing their tails. My God, what kind of man convinces one group of terrorists to attack another group?"

Jack Grimaldi grinned. "Yeah, I just wish I were in there giving him a hand."

The general ran his palms through his thick gray hair and sighed. "We all do, son. Believe me. But any man who can do what he's accomplished already, probably doesn't need our help. His methods are the best yet."

Jack Grimaldi nodded. Sure, it was a hell of an achievement to get as far as Colonel Phoenix had gotten, but it was stretching the odds to the tearing point to hope he could get much further alone.

But where to look? How to get him that help?

21

"Hit the dirt! *Hit the dirt!*"

The two Zwilling Horde terrorists dived over the wall and landed face-down in the hard snowbank on the other side.

"Fine," Bolan said in English-accented German. "Now the next two. Go!"

Two more hardguys hefted their new Uzis and charged across the campground, leaping the short wooden wall near the HQ cabin. Then each stood up and brushed the snow from his clothing.

"Forget your damned clothing!" Bolan yelled at them. "Protect your gun. Tuck it close to your body when you go over the wall, then cradle it when you roll. Next two!"

Thomas Morganslicht watched from the porch of his cabin, raking his thick black hair into place with his fingers, then absently chewing on his fingernails again. Something was not right. He didn't know what it was exactly, but he had this sour, dizzy feeling, almost like seasickness. Perhaps just the excitement, he wondered. After all, today was the day. The day when the Zwilling Horde would demonstrate to the world its brilliance and commitment. In a few hours they would have their deadly prize. Then, within a few days, hundreds would die. Perhaps even thousands.

But still his stomach churned and twisted. Especially in the presence of this American. Last night had been particularly bad. He had not been able to relax more than a few minutes at a time, and when he did fall asleep the nightmare returned. A hooded figure, face of granite, fire shooting from his fingertips, horrible flames. Even thinking about it now caused his stomach to ache and he could feel the slick film of sweat coating his skin. It was absurd to think that this hooded figure had anything to do with this American soldier. Dreams were only dreams, a shuffling of images and fears. He had learned about them in the university, though he had not done well in that course. Tanya had to do some of his homework so he would not fail.

Yes, Tanya. Sweet, ever-present Tanya. She had always been there to help him, to explain things, to protect him. Even when he hadn't wanted her help she was there.

He glanced around the camp at all the early morning activity. Men huffing and puffing in the chilly mountain air, their breath steaming like farm horses. The snow was hard and crusty from the constant melting and freezing process, but the roads remained clear and dry. There would be no trouble with transportation today.

"Tuck your head!" Bolan yelled at Hermann, who dived over the wall and flopped miserably on his stomach in an effort to protect his bandaged hand.

Thomas watched Tanya walking across the camp, her boots crunching through the snow. Her long black hair was knotted into a tight bun and tucked under her wool cap. Combat style, that's what she called it. Her face was its usual porcelain cold. He smiled. She was so proud of her self-control, her haughty distance. And it was true she was almost supernaturally cool during the most threatening crisis. But he knew, too, how that pale face would soon burn with bloodlust when they were within range of their target. That was the only time she showed genuine passion.

"What's the American doing shouting orders at our men?" he rasped at her as she approached the porch.

"I told him to run the men through a few special drills. Don't worry, he knows what he's doing. We should take advantage of his knowledge."

"You haven't forgotten our decision to kill him after this is over, have you?" he whispered.

"On the contrary," she smiled. "I want you to do your best work on him. Exceed yourself. I want what you did to those two agents to look like kindness. There should not be one square inch of his body left unexplored that might cause him excruciating pain. And not just pain, I want you to humiliate him however you can, physically, psychologically. Get Rudi to help you, I'm sure he'd appreciate the opportunity. And then when our Sergeant Grendal reaches that limbo beyond pain, I want you to chop his body into bits—except for the head. That we want them to recognize. After they receive his remains the authorities will think twice about how they are to deal with us."

Thomas studied his sister's face with puzzlement. In the past she had not minded his torturing and brutalizing certain people, but she had never encouraged him either. Now she was *insisting* on it. He could tell by the hard edges around her mouth that she meant it, too. Whatever the American had done to earn her wrath, he would certainly be sorry by tonight. This would be Thomas's greatest achievement, perhaps making it last for days before death would end his pleasure...and the sergeant's life.

"What happened to Hermann's hand?" he said, nodding at the bandage.

"An accident."

Rudi came around the corner of one of the buildings and Thomas was startled at the man's appearance. Dark purple bruises circled his eyes and spread across his cheeks. His nose was bandaged with white adhesive tape, but it still looked as if it had been flattened with a sledgehammer.

"My God," Thomas gasped. "What happened to Rudi, his face?"

"An argument with the American. No one's fault."

"No one's fault! First Hermann has an 'accident,' then Rudi is injured. We should kill this American right now, not take any chances of taking him along."

"There's no rush," she said quietly. "He's a man who will do anything for money. He won't harm our mission. If we had more like him we could pull this whole thing off with half the men."

"I don't like it." Thomas shook his head. "He's dangerous."

Tanya smiled. "So are we, brother. So are we."

Bolan grabbed one of the hardguys roughly by the shoulder and pitched him forward into the snow. "Pick up your feet! All of you. You'll never make it through this kind of snow if you use your legs like plows. You'll poop out after half a mile.''

The terrorists grumbled but under the watchful eyes of Tanya and Thomas Morganslicht, dutifully picked up their feet and trudged forward.

Bolan continued shouting automatic orders at them while he studied the situation around him. Tanya had "suggested" he warm the troops up with some special drills, so he'd been making it look legitimate and military. It had been a clever move on her part. This way he was out in the middle of the campground, unarmed, his voice could be heard anywhere in the camp, and he was surrounded by armed killers. It was tighter security than locking him up.

Without looking directly at them, he was aware of Thomas and Tanya conversing on the porch of their cabin. He did not need to overhear their conversation to know exactly what they were saying. They were a little shorthanded after last night's raid, so they would take advantage of having this trained soldier. They had already offered him money, and since that was what they thought he wanted most in the world, there would be no suspicion of betrayal. Nevertheless, they had probably decided to kill him immediately after the raid, to avoid paying him, and choking off any risk that he might sell them out for a better offer. That gave Bolan until the raid to free the hostages and figure a way to grind these people into the dirt.

"All right," Thomas yelled as he approached Bolan, his Luger tucked into the waist of his jeans. "I think that's enough warm-up, Sergeant. Nicely done." He slipped into his friendly mask again, tugging the corners of his mouth into a parody of a smile. He waved at Rudi, who stood nearby scowling at Bolan. It was no longer hate in Rudi's eyes, but something more basic, an animal passion for revenge. With gun if possible, but with teeth and nails if necessary. Rudi pivoted, the morning sun glinting off his white bandaged nose, and hurried toward the cabin where the hostages were kept during the night.

Tanya joined her brother and Bolan. "It's too bad we didn't have you here earlier, Sergeant. You could have whipped these men into real shape for us."

"They'll do as is," Thomas protested.

Tanya sighed impatiently. "No one's questioning your ability as a trainer, Thomas. But Sergeant Grendal has had more experience in this sort of thing."

"Of course," Thomas acknowledged.

Bolan wiped the sweat from his forehead with

the back of his sleeve. "Well, I still might be interested in training them after today. We could work out a price per head, or maybe I could make you a deal on the whole lot."

Tanya smiled. "You never quit, do you? If there's a dollar to be made, you're in there pitching."

"Yeah, well, I'm just a small businessman trying to make a living."

"Naturally," Thomas nodded. "But after today we will no longer require your services. Once our mission is successful, we will pay you a reasonable fee for your work and then drop you off in Mannheim."

"And after that," Tanya added, "you're on your own."

"Suits me," Bolan smiled. "Just one question. I'd like to have an idea what I'm risking my neck for."

Tanya nodded at her brother and he began to speak, pacing slightly as he did. "The key, of course, Sergeant Grendal, is to have the most possible impact for the least possible exertion. The best way to achieve this is to show the world we mean business in a big way."

"Such as?"

"Such as killing several hundred people at once. A large bomb of some sort would be most effective, perhaps in a movie theater, or a hospital." He stopped, gnawed on a stubborn thumbnail, and continued. "But as terrifying as random bombings are, they don't have the impact that will make our Soviet and Arab friends sit up and take notice. So my sister came up with an even better idea," he said creepily. "We bought some interesting information two months ago, probably originally sold by someone not unlike yourself."

"Yes," Tanya added, "unscrupulous and money-grubbing."

"The information cost us dearly, most of what we'd saved after the last three robberies. But it was worth it." He paused to smile mysteriously. "We have learned that today, in just—" he looked at his watch "—six hours and twenty-seven minutes, your army will begin transporting a certain deadly shipment for delivery to a NATO research base in Hamburg. The cargo—yellow rain."

Bolan's face tensed, his teeth clenched hard. He could feel a chill working its way along his neck and through his scalp. "Are you crazy? That stuff's bad news. Unless you know *exactly* what you're doing, it will backfire on you."

"We aren't afraid," Tanya said.

"Then you're not too smart," Bolan shot back. "Maybe you don't know enough to be scared. Just ask some of the people in Laos and

Afghanistan, where your Soviet mentors tried it out. Ask them about the choking, the blood vessels that burst inside you so that the whole body becomes a huge hemorrhage. It's one of the most agonizing deaths ever devised. And that's the stuff you want to fool around with?"

"We know all that, Sergeant," Tanya said. "And we are not so foolish as to not take precautions. We know how to handle the substance and we know how to administer it when the time comes. A simple aerosol device should spread enough to kill several hundred people at a playground, say."

"Children?" Bolan asked quietly.

"Of course. There is nothing more terrifying than the loss of children. One need only look at the panic in your own Atlanta with the slaughter of the black children. The public outcry almost brought down the city government. Imagine how much power we will have once we've killed off a few hundred. After that, they will beg to meet our demands."

Bolan stared at the two of them, controlling his mounting urge to kill them right now. He could do it, too, before any of their followers even knew what had happened. His elbow crushing a windpipe, his palm shoving nose cartilage back into the brain. But that was not the way. Not yet.

Yeah, he knew all about "yellow rain." The Soviets had created it from wheat grains to form a weapon that kills whether you breathe it, eat it, or just touch it. One so deadly that there is no cure, no real prevention. That's why the army was taking it to the NATO compound for research. April had briefed him on the whole thing months ago when the first reports came in of the captured killer that some Afghan rebels had snagged away from the Soviets. The army hoped through research and analysis to find some way to combat it, some way to help those brave Afghan warriors fighting against all odds to free their homeland. They had no hope against such sophisticated murder. Besides, who knew how soon the Soviets might want to try using it elsewhere.

But somehow, as it always does, word got out about the transport activity, and now these vultures were preparing to swoop down and steal it. Once they had it, there was no way to stop them from killing whoever they wanted, whenever they wanted. And right now they wanted to kill children.

"Move!" Rudi hollered, thumping his wooden club against the ground as he led the ragged athletes across the camp. "I said move!" he screamed again, cuffing Udo Ganz on the back of the head.

"Not so hard, Rudi," Tanya cautioned. "We need his head clear for the skiing."

In the bright sunlight they looked much worse than they had before. Bolan noticed the drawn pale look to the face, the dark circles under the eyes, the pasty skin, dirty oily hair, and general hopelessness in their dull eyes.

Babette Pavlovski squinted with one hand shading her eyes as she looked toward Bolan standing with the twins. Her mouth twisted into a sneer and she looked quickly away. Udo Ganz merely looked frightened and confused, anxious to please his tormentors. Bolan didn't blame him his fear, he'd earned it. He had already proved his courage on the Olympic battlegrounds, and now he was completely out of his element.

The slim Oriental, Mako Samata, looked wan but otherwise peaceful within himself. Despite the circumstances, he walked with a slight swagger as if he were in complete control of the situation, waiting only to exercise his power. Bolan had to admire his style.

The last of the group was Clifford Barnes-Fenwick, the Welsh archer whose grief over his dead son might be the one thing to destroy everyone's chance of escape. The bruises around his swollen nose looked much less awesome when compared to the damage on Rudi's face.

As the hostages were lead out into the center of the camp, several of the troops hefted their Uzis and fanned out to form an armed perimeter.

There would be no attempted escapes during today's rehearsal.

"All right, you've done it before, let's see it again. But this time it must be perfect." Thomas towered over the wiry Oriental, but Mako projected the impression that he was the much taller man. Bolan noticed that Thomas kept a respectable distance between himself and Mako, even as he lectured the man. "Okay, now, Samata, you will be the first member of your team to operate. Do you understand?"

"I have understood from the beginning," he said with a contemptuous sigh.

"Then there will be no problem."

"Of course not. I am trained in the art of ninjutsu. Military bases are easier to penetrate than many private homes."

"Excellent," Thomas smiled. "But remember, we will have a hidden gun trained on you at all times. If you do manage to escape, we will immediately execute the rest of your friends."

"You have made yourself clear," Mako said.

"Fine. Now I want to see you demonstrate once again how quickly you can disable a man." He called over his shoulder at Rudi. "Clock him...now!"

Rudi clicked the stopwatch as Mako began his first move. It was obvious to Bolan this was the same course they'd had him working on for weeks. The goal was for him to knock out two guards that Thomas had planted in the far cabin. Both guards were armed and expecting an attack from Mako, only they did not know how or when it would come. By Bolan's estimate, it had taken Mako less than thirty seconds to vault the small wooden wall and disappear entirely from sight.

Everyone looked around for him, but he was nowhere to be seen. Thomas and Tanya exchanged nervous glances as if afraid he might have made a break for it.

Finally, Thomas looked at his watch, pulled out his Luger and walked briskly toward the cabin where the guards were waiting. He had taken no more than half a dozen steps when the front door of the cabin swung open and Mako stepped out with a bored expression on his face.

"They should regain consciousness in about two hours," he said to Thomas, walking past him without looking at him. He rejoined the other athletes who stood in the middle of the campground.

"Time?" Thomas asked Rudi.

"Three minutes, thirty-eight seconds."

Thomas beamed a genuine smile. "Excellent!" He turned to Clifford Barnes-Fenwick. "Now, Mr. Fenwick—"

"Barnes-Fenwick," the Welshman corrected.

"Yes, of course. We have given you ample opportunity to prove your worth to us. Your particular skills are necessary, but not indispensable. We know that there are hidden metal detectors and X-ray machines at our military target, screening all personnel who enter for concealed weapons. Now, your little Oriental buddy here will knock out the two guards at the gatehouse and turn off the detectors. You will be able to pass through the metal detector with your wooden bow and cover Mako until he's deactivated the detectors. Because of the silent nature of your weapon, no one will hear anything. But you may be required to shoot several people with very little time in between." He snapped his fingers at one of his troops. "Now the only question that remains is whether you still are capable of making such precision shots."

The hardguy he'd snapped at brought a thick wooden bow with a plastic arrow rack attached to the bow's handle and handed them to Clifford. The Welshman hesitated a moment, his hand halfway outstretched but afraid to touch them, as if he feared they were charged with a fatal dose of electricity. He looked over his shoulder at Bolan, looking deep into the big man's eyes. Bolan gave the slightest of nods with his eyes and Barnes-Fenwick suddenly snatched the bow and quiver out of the terrorists hands.

"I can make your bloody shots," he said with disgust. He studied the bow for a moment and shook his head unhappily. "This has only a fifty-pound pull. I should have preferred eighty to give me a little more distance."

"You won't need distance," Tanya said. "You have only a thirty-yard circumference to defend, and then only for a few minutes. After that the metal-detector alarm system will be off and our men will be there with their machine guns to take over." She placed her hands on her hips and addressed everyone around her. "I want to remind you all that this is our only opportunity to steal yellow rain. It is the only time the stuff will be outside the safety of high-security buildings. If you fail, the results will be tragic—for all of us. Therefore, anyone who is not doing their best job today will be shot immediately." She swung back to face the athletes, letting the threat hang in the air.

"Okay," Thomas said, clapping his hands as if to physically break his sister's spell. "Let's move on to the Pavlovski woman."

Babette stepped forward. Bolan was amazed at how startlingly attractive she was despite all the physical and mental hardships she had been through. Her face had the hard expression of a survivor, yet with the soft edges of a beautiful woman. He noticed how carefully Tanya studied her as she leaped smoothly atop the narrow wooden wall and stood there balanced as gracefully as if she were on solid ground. An involuntary frown of jealousy tugged at Tanya's mouth.

"You will do just as you have practiced," Thomas said, picking up a green canvas knapsack; it reminded Bolan of the kind the boy scouts used to carry when he was a kid. "There are the same two bricks in here, approximating the weight of the cannister you will be carrying." He handed the knapsack to her, which she quickly slipped onto her back. "Now, there is a ten-foot-high wall that runs parallel to the surrounding fence for twenty feet before curving back around one of the buildings. Once the cannister has been handed to you by either my sister or myself, you are to climb that wall and run along it until you see Rudi waiting on the other side. When you spot him, you are to toss the entire pack over the fence to him. Clear?''

"Quite,'' Babette snapped.

"Good, now let me see you run this wall as fast as you can.''

She glared at him with burning defiance, as if deciding whether or not to throw the knapsack in his face. But finally her shoulders sagged in acceptance and she nodded affirmatively.

"Go!'' Thomas shouted.

Babette Pavlovski, once Czechoslovakia's prima donna gymnast, dashed across the rickety wooden wall like a sprinter. The fact that the wall was only four inches wide did not slow her in any way. She covered the distance in only a few seconds, her sneakered feet slapping wood in a breathless rhythm. When she reached the end of the wall she leaped off and landed lightly on the ground.

"Yes,'' Thomas nodded happily. "Very good. I'm quite pleased.''

"Well, that just makes my day,'' Babette said, shrugging off the knapsack and dropping it on the ground.

Thomas ignored her and turned to face his sister.

"That leaves only Mr. Barnes-Fenwick to display his ability,'' she reminded Thomas.

Tanya strolled up to the Welshman and stared into his battered face. "This will be your final opportunity to live, Welshman. Your skills would give us the few extra seconds that could make a difference. But if you aren't there, we will just have to take our chances. You will never know how it all turns out, because you'll already be dead." She turned and walked away. "It's up to you."

Clifford watched her with his sad, tired eyes, and Bolan feared that he might simply drop the bow and stroll away. If he did, Bolan had no doubt that Tanya would kill him right then and there. If he could not help in the assault, at least dead he would serve as a warning to the others. But that was the Welshman's decision. Bolan could not help him if he chose to die. There were the others to consider.

The archer took a deep breath and grasped the bow firmly in his left fist. He snapped the black wooden arrow from the plastic quiver and notched it into the string. It was a hunting arrow, with razor edges and barbs to keep the arrow from being pulled out once it penetrated flesh.

"We also have a glove for your right hand," Thomas said, "and rubber balls to silence the string when it's released."

"I don't need the glove," he said, tugging

slightly on the string to get a feel for the tension. "As for the sound of the string, well, there'll be enough surface noise to cover that anyway. So let's get on with it. What are my targets?"

Thomas shot a self-satisfied grin at Tanya, who remained coolly aloof as she watched the proceedings.

"Those three cabin doors," he said, pointing at the cabins lined up on one side of the camp. The farthest was fifty yards, the closest twenty-five yards. "Let me see how quickly you can hit each door. *If* you can—"

But before he could finish his sentence, the Welsh archer was already moving. He pulled the string back to his cheek and released, sending the thin shaft whistling at the farthest door. It struck with a thud and twang. But by then he was already firing at the next target. And then the next. Each struck home, all within five seconds of the first shot.

"Amazing!" Thomas said. "Incredible."

But while Thomas continued to praise the shot, Bolan noticed something else. A look in the Welshman's eye. It was a look not many people would recognize, it required a specialized kind of training and experience. It isn't everybody who can tell when a man is getting ready to kill. It's a flicker, really, a darkening of the iris, a grimness around the mouth that reveals that a heavy decision has been made, one that cannot be reversed.

That was the look Bolan saw in Clifford as he watched the archer casually ease another arrow from the quiver as if to get ready for the next trick shot. Trick shot, yeah, one that would end up sticking out of Thomas Morganslicht's chest. And he would probably get another one into Tanya, too, before the surrounding hardguys pumped a couple hundred rounds into him. And into the rest of the athletes. And into Mack Bolan.

The archer notched his arrow and tightened his three-fingered grip around the string. He started to raise the bow.

Bolan stepped forward and grabbed the bow. "Hey, I used to hunt a little with a bow. These arrows don't look long enough."

"Don't be an idiot, Sergeant," Thomas said angrily. "You can see for yourself they'll do just fine."

Clifford tried to pull the weapon free from Bolan's iron grip. "Leave me alone," he growled in a low whisper.

"I don't know," Bolan said loudly. "Arrows have to be measured according to each man's pull. These look a little short."

"Would you please shut up," Tanya said. "Mr. Barnes-Fenwick doesn't seem to mind.

Rudi, take the bow and escort our guests back to their room. We want them to get plenty of rest before this afternoon.''

Rudi elbowed Bolan aside and jerked the bow out of the Welshman's hand. Bolan smiled grimly with relief, but Clifford scowled at him in frustrated rage.

"What about the skier?'' Thomas asked. "Shouldn't we run him through one more time?''

"I think not. He's done it perfectly every day, so there's no need to wear him out so soon before the real thing. He knows the route and he can make the jump off the mini-ramp that we have already constructed.'' She addressed Udo. "You can drop the knapsack in the truck as it passes under you?''

"Yes,'' Udo said nervously. "I have not missed once so far.''

"Fine. Then once you've dropped it, you can keep skiing to freedom.''

"With the army chasing after him instead of you,'' Bolan added.

She smiled smugly. "Yes, but it's still a chance for him to live. Now, you help Rudi lock our little Olympians back in their room. The cabin, not the garage. We want them ready. We have only hours to go.''

Rudi pounded his club against the ground.

"Let's go," he roared and the four athletes began to shuffle away in a loose line.

They had not gone ten yards before Babette tripped and pitched face-first into the snow. Bolan reached over, grabbing her elbow to help her up, but as she rose she whirled around and pushed him away.

"Don't touch me, you pig!" she yelled, pushing him away. But as she struggled against him, their faces only inches away, she looked up at him, and with the briefest of movements, winked at him.

Then he knew for sure that she would be ready for the break, whenever it came. The slaps had been part of her act, an act so convincing he hadn't been sure himself.

"Get away!" she hollered, brushing the snow from her jacket and marching on.

Bolan looked over his shoulder at the terrorist twins. Thomas merely looked annoyed. But Tanya, obviously pleased, was smiling her thin, evil smile.

22

"How much longer?" Bolan asked from the back of the van.

"Twenty more minutes, Sergeant," Tanya answered.

Once again Bolan found himself in the lead van with Tanya driving and Rudi riding shotgun, cradling the same 12-gauge Stevens shotgun he had used the night before on the Black Sunday raid. Bolan had the same H & K G-11 balanced across his knees, and Tanya still had the remaining clips.

The big difference was that instead of being filled with terrorists like it had been last night, the van was filled with four ex-Olympic champions on their way to the hellgrounds of horrific death, the doomland of chemical fire.

The grotesque Rudi kept his shotgun leveled on them from the front of the bus, and another faceless hardguy kept his Uzi pointed at them from the back of the van.

Through the rear window, Bolan could see

Thomas behind the wheel of the trailing van and Hermann sitting next to him. And crowded behind them in the back of their van were ten hardened killers stroking Uzis, sweating and dreaming and praying it would be their buddy and not them that gets killed.

Whatever was going to go wrong had to go wrong soon. They were less than twenty minutes from the hardsite and Bolan could not wait until they arrived there. First, he wanted these animals nowhere near striking range of that "yellow rain." Second, with all the excitement, he wanted to avoid soldiers firing innocently on the hostages. And third, he wanted to prevent Clifford from having to fire arrows into any unsuspecting guards...although he had an idea that the Welshman had no intention at all of killing anyone, at least anyone outside the Zwilling Horde.

Bolan tried to catch Mako's eye, but the slim Oriental stared straight ahead as if in a self-induced trance.

"That was quite a stunt you pulled back there at the camp," Bolan told him.

Mako glanced at the big American and nodded. "Child's play."

"Perhaps you just need a more challenging situation." Bolan let his stare penetrate Mako's eyes.

Mako shifted on his seat, seemed to understand the message beneath the words. "Perhaps."

"Shut up!" spat Rudi, waving his shotgun between Bolan and Mako.

Bolan could not be sure that Mako had understood him, had caught the movement of the eyes that assigned the guy with the Uzi to him. But there was no more time to decide. If they were ever going to make their move it would be now.

And so it was.

Bolan lunged forward, using his left forearm to drive the barrel of the shotgun toward the floor, using the butt of the H & K to club Rudi's skull. Even as he was still grabbing at the shotgun he saw Mako leap across the van at the terrorist with the Uzi.

The van wobbled from the shifting of weight, but it wobbled even more when the butt of Bolan's gun cracked Rudi's skull, causing the giant to emit a curdled cry as he impulsively pulled the trigger of his shotgun. The blast tore a hole in the floor. Tanya swerved the van, struggling to maintain control with one hand, reaching for her 9mm Firebird with the other.

Bolan was still grappling with Rudi when he saw Mako and Babette rush forward. Mako grabbed Tanya's wrist between his thumb and forefinger and applied enough pressure to snap the wrist. There was no mistaking that cracking sound coupled with her scream of pain. He yanked her out of the driver's seat while Babette deftly slid in behind the wheel, flooring the gas pedal.

Rudi still clung to the shotgun, trying to wrench it out of Bolan's grip. His huge yellow horse teeth flashed in a grimace of pain and concentration, but he was already too weak from the blows to the head. With a sudden twisting movement, Bolan pulled the shotgun free and swung it around to face Rudi.

"I am unarmed," Rudi pleaded. "You would not shoot an unarmed man."

"You've been watching the wrong movies, guy," Bolan said, and fired into the giant's face a 12-gauge boxcar with death as the freight. Ragged chunks of flesh bloodied the inside of the windshield. Fringe pellets shattered the window of the passenger's door.

"God!" Babette shouted and the van swerved before she got it under control.

Bolan swung around to face the back of the van. Mako hovered over Tanya, the 9mm Firebird pointed at her chest.

The terrorist toughguy lay sprawled on the

floor, his eyes wide open, his neck floppily distorted from being broken by an expert.

Clifford Barnes-Fenwick gripped the dead man's Uzi with a stranglehold as if uncertain who to turn it on.

Udo Ganz remained seated where he'd been, staring blankly through the hole in the floor as the road rushed like rapids beneath the speeding van.

"All right, listen to me," Bolan said. "I'm going to tell you what to do and you're going to do it without question or argument. In about thirty seconds, Babette will stop this van. That will force the van behind us to stop too. I'll stall them long enough for you to tear the hell out of here. They will not be able to follow you."

"You against twelve of them?" Babette protested.

"I'll have her," he replied, nodding at Tanya.

"You fool," Tanya snarled. "We could have made you wealthy. A wealthy idiot."

"The only thing you were going to make me is deceased."

"Why can't we just shoot it out," the Welshman boomed. "We could shoot out their tires and keep going. We have guns too."

"Because they have more guns," Bolan said

simply. He did not want to tell them that their safe escape was only a minor corollary to his main mission, which was the total destruction of the Zwilling Horde. No, the Executioner didn't want to escape. "Now stop the van."

Babette hesitated, began pumping the brakes until the van slowed down. When the speedometer showed less than twenty kilometers an hour, she eased it off the road onto the icy shoulder.

Thomas's van followed suit, slowing and pulling off the road and parking twenty yards behind them. Bolan could see their exhaust pumping into the chilly air.

"Cut the motor," he told Babette.

She turned the motor off but left the key in the ignition. "Udo, you'll have to drive, I'm too nervous, Udo!"

"Of course," he said and climbed forward to the driver's seat.

"Okay, they've cut their engine," said Bolan. "Now, I'm going outside to talk. When you think you're ready to go, go! Start her up and drive like hell."

"I'm as handy with a gun as I am with my hands," Mako said quietly.

Bolan was touched by the slender man's subtle offer. He had proven himself a lion of a man already, but his skills would be better used helping the others escape. "I'll bet there's not a whole lot you *aren't* good at, guy. But this one's a solo."

Mako nodded understanding and gave a look of such sincerity that it expressed more friendship than a dozen speeches.

"Let's go, Sweet Pea," Bolan said, grabbed Tanya under the arm and hoisted her to her feet. "Toss me those clips." Udo threw Bolan two clips for the H & K. Bolan slipped one into place over the muzzle and looked back to the man. "You keep the Uzi, you may need it if I don't stop them." He slid open the VW side door and stepped out, pulling Tanya behind him. He looked back into the van at the brave band of athletes and smiled. "Good luck," he said, then slid the door closed with an echoing thud.

He dug the barrel of the H & K into the back of Tanya's skull while guiding her forward with his left hand. "Just stay cool, Commander," he whispered. "You wouldn't like what a couple rounds from this baby would do to your pretty little head."

"The only thing I don't like is *your* head," she hissed.

"Maybe, but right now your head is mine. I have it." He took a careful step, used the corner of the van for cover. "Come on out, Morganslicht," Bolan called. "New deal."

"That's an American phrase, FDR's New Deal?" Thomas was crazed with uncertainty.

"Yeah, this is going to be just like that."

The side door of the other van slid open and four armed hardguys jumped out, leveled their guns at Bolan. Then the front doors opened, Thomas and Hermann stepped out either side, and remained standing behind the metal doors.

"What happened, Tanya?" Thomas asked. There was a slight taunting in his voice, like he was pleased to see his sister screw up.

Bolan pressed the gun harder against her skull. "I'll do the talking for now."

"What do you want?" Thomas called.

"A bigger cut for one thing. And a permanent position in your organization. I think Rudi's position might be open." What was taking Udo so long? Now was the time to pull out, while half of them were out of the van.

The motor coughed once, caught, and the van lurched forward, squealing against the ice as it shot into the narrow road.

Thomas leaped back to his seat to give chase.

"Forget them," Tanya ordered her brother. "We will have another time. Now we must just regroup and replan."

Thomas watched as the van roared down the road, glancing anxiously back and forth between his sister and the disappearing van.

Finally he climbed back out. "I am sorry, Tanya," he said, "but we are too close for that now." He pulled his Luger from his shoulder holster and fired three slugs into his sister's chest.

Bolan shoved her forward at Thomas's first movement, fired a full automatic burst into both tires of the van before diving over the embankment, tucking the H & K close to his chest as he rolled ten feet down the other side into the underbrush and the thick dark forest.

"Get him!" Thomas screamed. Ten armed men jumped over the embankment, sliding after the American.

Bolan dodged out from behind a pine tree and caught two of the hardguys as they hit the bottom of the embankment. He sprayed a hailstorm of bullets across their groins, cutting them almost in half at the legs. They collapsed in heaps, their guts steaming as they were exposed to the cold air.

It was time to run, to weave back and forth behind trees, to lure them deeper into the forest. The deeper he went, the thicker the woods and the darker the atmosphere. He became the nightfighter once more, man of stealth and silence and cunning. The terrorists were spreading out farther and farther from one another, making Bolan's strategy inevitable.

He caught their point man all alone from behind, and using his garrote, choked the man
until eyes and tongue bulged out of his head.

The second man he surprised by silently leaping out from behind a tree, thrusting his stilet-
to into the startled man's stomach, twisting it
until he found the spine. He quietened the
dying victim with a suffocating grasp around
the face.

Bolan headed deeper into the woods, deeper
into the hellground, full tilt. The forest whip-
ping by him stank of moist undergrowth. It
was good here for the Executioner.

In some dark spot real soon, he would show
the light. The light of the truth—that to kill a
terrorist is not vengeance or cruelty, it is just
common sense. . . .

The public truth.

For, of course, it is the public who is most
exposed.

He sprinted ahead, cradling the caseless G-11
in a relaxed midriff sweep. Its plastic-molded
housing was a bizarre—even glorious—feature
among these trees, its loud modern streamlin-
ing a brave stab at circumstances already too
far gone.

As Bolan soft-soled it from pockets of dark
places to even gloomier spaces in the steaming
woods, the gun was soundless. Every tick and

rattle of its engineering was completely baffled by the casing, itself almost weightless in the superb balance of Bolan's flying grip. Gun and man—their noiselessness allowed the man the nice advantage of surprise.

He heard clues to the positions of his pursuers. Glaring clues, for they were playing a different game. They were snapping a twig or two, calling out, cursing once or twice. Very precise for Bolan. And he was already a football field ahead of them, ready for a stadium performance, listening in as tight as he could get it—reaching with the ear as far as a human can and them some—to score a victory. That was Bolan's game.

He knew the game was on, the minute he saw the hut. Right there in his path. Now victory was inevitable.

The hut was made of round pebbly rock. It was covered with a dense disguise of vine, thriving greenery, and sported a quaint but decaying Bavarian roof. Two windows, one on either side, one low entrance—holes in the wall. . . gaping square sockets. Perfect.

And better yet, this helpful litle edifice—blessed with that true and dramatic magic that we know as *timeliness*—was further blessed by its position, now perfect after many years, a little woodman's storage hut lying neglected all these years in wait. In wait, slap bang in the middle of the advancing line of shooting clowns.

Hot brother, little architecture! Bolan tapped the top of the small doorway as he ducked into the hut. Its floor was thick with undergrowth. Light from the windows on either side came through in a band between waist and head height. It was dank in the hut, but great. The ideal spot for the extraterrestrial action that Bolan had in mind. The action that isn't there when you look at it.... The action that plays somewhere else.

The kind of action that calls up the barrel of the Heckler and Koch assault weapon like an eagle on the wing, breathtaking in the easy way it rose, its only real weight aside from the magazine being its 1x scope, which now beaded in on its first visible target. Light as light waves, true as fate. Bolan shot the scum soldier who was in his sights at last.

Swiveling around instantly in the cramped hideout, arriving at a proper aim within the crack of the first shot, Bolan fired another short round out of the opposite window. His second visible target fell.

Bolan swung back to check the accuracy of his first shot. Empty woods showed where the target had been. But visible in the nearer view was a punk trooper taking aim, an anonymous shootist of the Zwilling Horde, a being with no love for life and therefore of no worth, a man prepared to waste his lousy existence on a dumb move. A really dumb last move.

The terrorist fired east across the distance that he guessed would end with the rifle that was doing the killing.

But the position was entirely wrong for that. The Executioner could have told him such data for a dime. . . if he had wanted a dime from the punk. And anyway, the guy never asked. Instead he fired that shot across the bows of the advancing Zwilling Horde, or damn near what remained of it, and he killed his brother soldier forty feet to the left of him.

The shot scored a random neck hit. The throat of the soldier, who shrieked with shock through shattered vocal cords—the sound of terror rebounding—pulsed out blood in red waterfalls. He was dead by the time his body had fallen to its knees. His head flopped expressionless on his shoulder, the gaping throat-hole soon a silent scream, a mockery of communication in an army too sick from the start to deserve any right to speak. Bolan watched the action discreetly from the edge of the window, his own silence a mark of strategic superiority.

The dead soldier had a companion next in

line, a terrorist now exposed from the thick cover of trees, who was in panic. His reaction to the death at his side was to start shooting. He aimed his bulky automatic over the falling head, spewing in terror the gun's tumbling issue in all directions.

One of those directions included a motionless target—the terrorist who had fired that last killing shot, now frozen in his tracks from some profound horror at his own act, even as hot lead screamed about him. Three shredders immediately found his flesh and did their work. The bullets ripped apart the back of his combat clothing as they exited like hurtling meat grinders.

Bolan dived out through the doorway of his sanctuary, firing the H & K in its max-round mode to take out the remaining terrorist on the left wing and then, spinning round to repeat history, to hit the remaining guy far on the right wing. The two opposing punks each showed puffs of pink mist as their backs exploded from the intercepted lead.

Six dead. Two killed by shots from their own side. A major encounter, yeah, made easy only by the bloody skills of an anguished man—by the Executioner unleashed. It had looked fast and furious. But in the deep inner Valhalla of his mind, where the numbers rose and fell, it had been a perilously slow killing for Mack Bolan. The plan had been spontaneous, dependent on the luck of the land and how it lay, and he was damn glad to get that witless help from the rattled killers who wiped each other out. Thanks guys. Thanks little hut.

He began circling back to the road, to the crippled van. He ran fast again, fleet as a high wind, silent as a breeze, almost invisible in his khaki army garb.

He had to get away from the graveyard of these woods. Bursting sprays of blood had defiled the natural order here. Bolan needed the road, needed direction for his continuing tormented last mile.

He was halfway there when he heard a sudden exchange of automatic gunfire. So Thomas's and Hermann's wait at the van was proving eventful. Excellent. What could be happening there?

Hunched over his H & K, he ran silently through the German woods.

Another chatter of gunfire and Bolan speeded up, ignoring the branches that lashed his eyes and the tangled underbrush that grabbed at his feet. Within minutes he was close enough to see who was shooting.

Babette Pavlovski.

Hermann and Thomas had her pinned down at the top of the embankment, just over the lip of the ridge. She was laid out flat against the incline, her feet dug into the snow to keep her from sliding down. At the rate her Uzi was spitting whizzers at the van, she'd be out of bullets before too long.

Bolan swung around behind her and slipped up the embankment, flopping into the snow next to her.

"What the hell are you doing here?" he demanded.

She fired another burst toward the van before answering. "I made them let me out about a half mile down the road. A quick jog and here I am."

"I told you to stay together and keep going."

A line of bullets from Thomas's gun thudded into the ground a foot in front of them, kicking a powder of snow into their faces.

"I do what is right, not what I'm told."

Bolan liked this woman. Now he studied the situation with a quiet detachment. Hermann was standing behind the van, peeking out occasionally to fire at them. Thomas was squatting behind the passenger's seat, popping up to fire through the open window, using the open door as a shield.

"Okay, this time do *exactly* as I tell you. And I mean exactly, do you understand?" Bolan smiled.

"Yes," she answered.

"I want you to keep firing at them, but only in three-round bursts, and only at ten-second intervals." Now he was as serious as death.

"What are you going to do?" she asked.

"Whatever it takes," he said, and slid back down the embankment. He had to hurry. He had to kill them. There had been enough of them and it was over now.

He gave a good one-eighth of a mile berth before rising up the embankment again, far behind the van. He crept closer, waiting for the good shot. Hermann stopped moving, long enough to change clips, and Bolan dropped to one knee and brought him into his crosshairs. Hermann fumbled with the new clip because of his bandaged hand. Less than a second later he was dead, his face resculpted where three bullets had chiseled away his jaw and cheek.

"Hermann!" Thomas screamed from inside as Bolan covered the rest of the distance between him and the van.

Thomas kept firing from the van, increasing the tempo now, his gun blazing blindly in Babette's direction. Wisely she did not panic, stuck to the three-round, ten-second firing pattern.

Behind the van, Bolan was stripping the shirt from Hermann's back, shredding it into long strips and shoving them down into the gas tank. He allowed just enough hanging out to give him a running headstart. When he heard Babette's next three-round blast, he ignited the cloth and high-stepped it away. Then Bolan gripped the H & K in both hands and fired a burst into the side of the van.

Thomas swung around to face this new onslaught, his eyes wide with terror and despair. He lifted his Uzi to take aim at Bolan when a sound from hell ripped through his ears.

The van's gas tank exploded, shooting a tidal wave of roaring fire from one end of the van to the other. Thomas's flaming body was hurtled through the windshield, where it snagged on the sharp glass, trapping his burning flesh in the flames.

"Babette!" Bolan called, and she pulled herself to her feet and ran to him, a sickened expression on her face.

"Oh, God. Oh, my God," she moaned as she watched Thomas's impaled and writhing body sizzle into something unrecognizable.

"Never mind him," Bolan snapped. "It's better than he deserved."

Bolan retrieved his holstered Beretta from the smoking corpse, then pulled Babette to her feet and led her down the road at a slow jog.

Yeah, he thought, glancing over his shoulder at the flaming van and scattered bodies, at

Tanya's limp and lifeless shape, sometimes the debts do get paid.

In full.

"And his enemies shall lick the dust," said Bolan to himself, quoting Psalm 72, the Psalm for Solomon. That is certainly true, he thought, turning to face the open road, in the drizzle just starting, the foul weather of Europe so full of the feeling of history, as he went on with his fateful mile.

Mission complete in full.

Now back to Jack.

And to America, thank God.

A thick conspiracy had been unraveled in the space of a few heartbeats. That is all it took. Months of planning, and terror, and humiliation had preceded Mack Bolan's arrival, had—unawares—awaited the tumbling of the numbers.

For when the Executioner hit, he hit fast. The complications were reduced to threads of traumatized tissue in seconds.

Hit and git. The American way.

Forget those goddamned complications.

Don Pendleton's

MACK BOLAN

THE EXECUTIONER SERIES

*There are times when a man will make his stand
for what is right. To be truly alive, you must be
ready to die. More difficult still, there are times
when you have to be willing to kill. I am both
ready to die and willing to kill.*

—Mack Bolan, a.k.a. Col. John Phoenix,
THE EXECUTIONER

Don Pendleton had been a navy radioman, a rail-
road telegrapher, an air-traffic controller, and
an aerospace engineer when he turned to full-
time writing. His book originally entitled *Duty
Kill* was subsequently published as *The Executioner: War Against the Mafia*. It was the first
Mack Bolan novel, and the introduction of an
entirely new genre—that of the Aggressor, the
one-man army dedicated to the eradication of
society's enemies by whatever means necessary.

As Pendleton has pointed out, Mack Bolan never actively sought the role of Aggressor. Bolan earned the name The Executioner for his successful handling of dangerous and delicate sniper missions behind enemy lines. But when he returned home, he discovered that (in his own words) he had been fighting the wrong war. Thus, with a spray of rapid fire from a game rifle, began the incredible one-man crusade that brought him to his peak of action as John Phoenix, the free world's top anti-terrorist, a fighter for our freedom from fear. The measure of public support that The Executioner has earned is unique. In a time when people often feel helpless, without control over their lives, the vision of a being such as Mack Bolan who is the essence of independent man is a powerful and appealing one, vastly successful in terms of reader enjoyment and loyalty. Bolan is not a superman; he is a warrior who achieves magnificent results in extreme situations, and he achieves them in an entirely realistic manner. He remains at the far forefront of all heroic-adventure writing.

"Do not assume that the masculine myth is in danger of extinction...Mack Bolan [was created] to dignify the American fighting man. Lines crackle on every page!"

—*Toronto Star*

MACK BOLAN

THE EXECUTIONER 47

Renegade Agent

Coming in November from Gold Eagle Books

Treason is the target of Mack's body-shredding hellfire when a busted CIA agent starts trafficking with terrorists in Europe. The ante goes real high when this turncoat scum takes a hostage....

Mack's task: eliminate every one of the bastards involved. He blows the hell out of an armament factory in New England, flattens a munitions warehouse at London's Heathrow airport, then breaches the traitor's base and brings hell on earth in a firerain of explosive action.

Watch for *Renegade Agent*, Executioner #47, wherever paperbacks are sold—November 1982. Also new Able Team and Phoenix Force books—watch for details!

"Mack Bolan's struggle is a personification of the struggle of collective mankind from the dawn of time. He is a consecration of the life principle. He proclaims that life is meaningful, that the world is important, that it does matter what happens here—that universal goals are being shaped on this cosmic cinder called Earth.

"The guy cares. The whole world is Bolan's family. He reacts to the destructive principle inherent in the human situation, and he's fighting it. The goons have rushed in waving guns, intent on raping, looting, pillaging, destroying. And he is blowing their damn heads off, period, end of philosophy. And that is a high and heroic idea."

—*Don Pendleton*